19 TILL I DIE

Anjali Kirpalani is the bestselling author of the novels *Never Say Never* and *Written in the Stars*. Born in India, she lived in South Africa for eight years before returning to Mumbai. She has been a Radio Jockey, TV anchor with ET NOW and the editor of Stylekandy.com, a fashion portal. Anjali has written several successful radio dramas for the SABC (South African Broadcasting Corporation). While studying at the University of KwaZulu Natal in South Africa, Anjali received the opportunity to be an exchange student for a semester at the University of Guelph in Canada, an opportunity she will always cherish. *19 Till I Die* is her ode to the best year of her life.

She can be reached on anjalikkirpalani@gmail.com

Alternatively, connect with her on any of the following social media platforms:

Facebook: Anjali Kirpalani

Twitter/Instagram: anjalikir

AF632396

19 TILL I DIE

ANJALI KIRPALANI

HarperCollins *Publishers* India

First published in India by
HarperCollins *Publishers* in 2018

Building 10, Tower A, 4th Floor, DLF Cyber City, Phase II,
Gurugram Haryana- 122002, India

www.harpercollins.co.in

2 4 6 8 10 9 7 5 3 1

Copyright © Anjali Kirpalani 2018

P-ISBN: 978-93-5277-616-0
E-ISBN: 978-93-5277-617-7

This is a work of fiction and all characters and incidents described in this book are the product of the author's imagination. Any resemblance to actual persons, living or dead, is entirely coincidental.

Anjali Kirpalani asserts the moral right to be identified as the author of this work.

All rights reserved. No part of this publication may be reproduced, stored in a retrieval system, or transmitted, in any form or by any means, electronic, mechanical, photocopying, recording or otherwise, without the prior permission of the publishers.

Typeset in 11/14.5 Sabon LT Std by
R. Ajith Kumar

Printed and bound at
MicroPrints India, New Delhi

To those who are young, and those who are young at heart.

'Ask the young. They know everything.'
– Joseph Joubert

PART 1

JANUARY

ZAID

'I'm at Musgrave Centre, baby. I'll be at yours in five minutes, okay? I love you.'

'No, no! Don't come now. I … um … we've got relatives over.'

Devina sounds panicked.

I glance at my watch. It's 11 a.m. Considering Devi's family isn't that close-knit, it's odd that she should have callers so early on a Saturday morning. Her behaviour has been weird these last few weeks. She arrived in Durban only last night and we haven't seen each other in a week. Surely, she should be keen to see me? I can't shake the feeling that something is wrong.

I pay for the sequined dress, which she said she wanted the last time we walked past Edgar's. When the cashier returns my credit card, something makes me ask her what their return policy is.

'Thirty days.' She smiles.

I nod my thanks, collect the bag and receipt and rush

out of the store. A short drive up the road and I reach Devi's place in under five minutes. I park my car in front of her building. Just as I reach for the buzzer, I spot the electric gate opening and her neighbour, Mrs David, emerges and smiles at me. She has seen me around often enough to know that I'm not a shady lurker. I smile back; hoping that my calm exterior doesn't give away the tension coiled within me.

I pause for a moment outside Devina's door summoning the nerve to knock. A few seconds later, I hear a muffled voice. 'Baby, you came! Let me, just … just give me a minute, okay?'

She opens the door three minutes later. I know because I timed it on my watch.

'Hi, baby!' she says and hugs me. Her face is flushed.

'I know you said you had guests at home, but I simply had to see you. I hope your parents won't mind.'

'They're all in the living room. I don't think this is a good time. Why don't I meet you in an hour, somewhere?' she says, blocking the doorway.

I stare into her eyes and she looks away. I don't even need to hear it from her. I already know what's going on. I push past her and walk into the apartment. It's eerily quiet. There's no sign of Mr and Mrs Naidoo, let alone the visiting 'relatives'. I open the door to the en-suite bathroom.

Although I was expecting it on some level, nothing has prepared me for the sight that meets my eyes. Standing in her bathtub is a tall, muscular guy. Wrapped around his waist is the white Turkish towel that I had gifted to Devi on her previous birthday (in case you're wondering, it was one amongst seventeen other gifts; I'm not a cheapskate). The towel reads 'Princess' and if I hadn't just discovered that my girlfriend is a lying, two-timing bitch, I might have found this hilarious.

Devi follows me into the bathroom. 'I can explain. I'm so, so, sorry, baby. I just ... it was a moment of weakness ... Lyle is an old friend from school. We bumped into each other when I was in Jozi in October. We started talking and messaging ... I'm ... I don't know what to say. I never meant to hurt you.' She is crying now.

I gather myself enough to speak. 'You never meant to hurt me. I'm having a little difficulty believing that actually. And for fuck's sake don't call me "baby". It makes me sick! So, let me get this straight, this has been going on for two months and you call it a "moment" of weakness? I'm pretty sure two months comprise several thousands of "moments". And you could have come clean after any one of those "moments", but you didn't.'

'Hey, man. She feels bad enough as it is. Don't make it worse,' the douche in the tub says.

That does it. I walk right up to him and punch him in the face. He's about to retaliate when Devi intervenes.

'Lyle, no!'

She pulls me away.

'I ... I'm sorry, ba—I'm sorry. I know I'm an absolute bitch for doing this to you. You don't deserve it. I don't know what I was thinking. You've been so good to me. You're the best boyfriend I've ever had. I don't even know ...' She dissolves into sobs.

She looks so very vulnerable and I never could bear to see her cry. However, all I feel now is pure rage. All those times she didn't want to meet me claiming she was too tired or had to study for a test, she was probably studying this douchebag's perfectly sculpted body. Fuck. How the hell could I be so fucking stupid? I feel like the dumbest guy in the world.

I look at her once more in disgust and walk away. Then I turn around and fling the shopping bag at her.

'Here! I'd been saving to get you this dress that you had your heart set on. I should just return it, but I want you to have it. I want it to remind you of the manipulative whore you are whenever you look at it. Fuck you, Devina Naidoo.'

I slam the door behind me and walk out of the building. I get into my car and drive around the streets of Durban aimlessly for an hour. So, this is what it feels like to have your heart yanked out of your chest and stomped upon. I feel weirdly numb.

FEBRUARY

FIONA

'YOU DO THAT AGAIN, Kev, and I'll kick your ass,' I mumble, yanking the duvet back over my face.

'Relax, I don't give a damn whether you wake up or not. Dad sent me. It's twelve, you lazy ass,' Kevin replies.

Trust my brother to be the bearer of bad news. And here I was, dreaming about Gabriel Macht, the guy who plays Harvey Specter in *Suits*. I squint at the clock on the wall. Kev is right. It is high time I woke up. But perhaps just a few more minutes...

Oh, Harvey, you're so fine. Of course, I can go away for the weekend with you. I'll need to check with my dad, though ... Oh, God! Dad! I wake up with a start.

Twenty minutes later, I'm seated at the dining table with Mom, Dad, Kev and Grandma.

'Mmm ... this omelette is super yum, Mom,' I say through a mouthful of egg.

'I think it's too salty,' Grandma growls.

Mom is about to retaliate snappily, but Dad swiftly changes the subject.

'Fiona, how are your studies coming along? Are you still struggling with math?'

I sigh. 'I'm trying. Satish Sir says I'm getting better. I got 70 per cent in the mock test last Friday. I got some trigonometry questions wrong, so he's going to do an extra hour on that with me tomorrow.'

'My poor baby is working so hard. No wonder you find it so hard to wake up these days.' Mom reaches out and squeezes my hand.

'Oh, don't be dramatic, Rashmi. Fiona isn't the only child to have ever done her twelfth. It's like that for everyone,' my ever-practical father scoffs.

Kevin's gleeful snort deposits a crumb into his airway and he ends up choking on his hash browns. It's now my turn to sneer at him. Mom gently pats Kevin on the back. Kev, the attention-starved brat that he is, revels in all the fussing. I roll my eyes. Dad doesn't even seem to notice this near-death experience. Got to love Dad!

'Just stay focused and you'll be fine, Fiona. Mum, do you want some juice?' Dad asks Grandma.

'No, you know I fall ill whenever I drink anything cold. This juice is freezing.' Grandma glares at Mom.

Dad, Kevin and I glance in trepidation at Mom. However, Mom, usually quick to rise to the bait, doesn't bat an eye. She grabs a slice from the toast rack and proceeds to butter it. I'm taken aback and impressed by her restraint. I make a mental note to ask her about it.

It is at this juncture that I realize that my life has

become so uneventful that Mom and Grandma's exchanges are now interesting to me.

I wolf down the last of my omelette and rise from the chair.

'Okay, bye, family. Later!'

'Where are you off to?' Mom asks.

'To a party, of course! Relax, Mom. I'm off to the confines of my room to do what I do for hours on end every single day. Study.' I sigh gustily for effect. I know I'm a drama queen but the most critical academic examinations of one's life happen just once – provided one doesn't fail in them – therefore, the way I see it, I have a few more months left to milk the twelfth-standard situation.

'Aw, just a few more days, sweetie. Don't worry, this too shall pass. Grab a shower and freshen up. If you sit to study now, you'll only end up having a shower at night. And you'll make the bathroom all wet again. When Tulsi comes in today I want her to clean the bathroom properly and make sure it is dry. Go, shower! I'll make you coffee in the meanwhile...'

'No, Mom! I've just eaten. I'll shower in a bit, I promise. Okay, thanks. Bye!' I rush off before she launches into a tirade about my cavalier attitude towards personal hygiene.

Back in my room, I shut the door and flop on to the bed. I dial Sandhya's number.

'Yo. What you up to?'

'Been staring at one page from my calculus text book for like an hour now. I'm not even joking,' she says.

'At least you've started. I just woke up sometime back. And you know I faffed all of yesterday. I just can't get myself to study. Argh!'

'I hear you, man. When will this crap end? Anyhoo, did you watch *Suits* yesterday? I couldn't believe it! How could Mike do that to Harvey?'

'I know! Craziness! I want a new episode like now! Why do we have to wait until Tuesday?'

I spend the rest of the day eating every hour, taking twenty-minute 'TV breaks', messaging Sandhya and napping. As I fall asleep surrounded by my text books, I can feel Mom drawing my duvet over me and patting my head. I smile. Aside from my studies sucking the fun out of my existence, life is pretty perfect. Man, I'm really going to miss Delhi when I'm off to uni in September.

MARCH

TIA

I open the rear door of the Innova parked in front of my apartment building. '*Abhi toh party shuru hui hai*' is blasting from the speakers. The grumpy uncle from flat 301 gives me a disgusted look. I jump in and shut the door.

Armaan, Stan and Neha cheer in unison when I get in the car. Armaan is driving and Stan is in the passenger seat. Neha shares the backseat with me.

'Looking good, Ti,' Neha greets me.

'Why thank you, Nene. You too.'

I've always been a little chubby but I've recently lost five kilos and its begun to show. I've just spent twenty minutes examining myself in the mirror, thanks to my friends being late. My reflection revealed that colouring my hair auburn last month was a good call. I decided while checking myself out in the mirror that I'm happy with the way I look. Sure, I would have loved having flawless skin but considering the sporadic acne breakouts have been loyal companions since I turned thirteen, I guess they're not going anywhere. Thank God for foundation.

'Guys, keep it down! The watchman and neighbours will start complaining to my parents, ya.'

'No way! Velu likes us! He'll stand up for us.' Stan laughs.

I can't help but giggle. 'His name is Vinay. You're not allowed to call him Velu!'

'But you call him Velu! That's not fair. Guys, I think Tia has the hots for her watchman,' Stan retorts.

'Yuck! Shut up, Stan! Idiot!' I say.

'I think you're right, Stan. Ti definitely has a thing for her watchman. And remember the driver, Raju? On that trip to Lonavala? She wouldn't let any of us talk to him! She was the only one allowed to say anything at all to him,' Neha says.

'Shut up, bum! That was because he was my dad's office driver. I had strict instructions from Dad to treat him well and not bug him.'

'And that's why you went for a spin alone with him?' Armaan chips in.

'Ugh! I give up! You guys are disgusting!' I wrinkle my nose.

'Acha, anyway, tell us – Daily or Olive – where do you want to go, Ti?' Stan asks.

'Daily, for sure. Smitha and gang are also going to be there.'

'Cool, so that's settled. Daily it is. Sorry, Nene. If it gets boring, we'll go to Olive. Cool?' Stan addresses Neha.

'Fine. Since you guys have decided to go to Daily daily, I guess I have no option,' Neha says.

'Was that supposed to be funny? Aw, Nene. You're so cute,' Armaan teases.

Stan and I catch each other's eye in the rear-view mirror. I stifle a giggle. Armaan and Neha make it so obvious that they like each other. The flirting has been going on since we all became a 'group' three years ago. I've mentioned it to Neha and discovered that the reason she doesn't want to act upon her feelings is because she doesn't want to ruin the group dynamics in case Armaan and she break up. Typical Neha. She's a worrier. She doesn't enjoy the present because she's too busy thinking about the repercussions in the future. Naturally, she thinks I don't plan enough for my future. I am the only one in our group who doesn't really have any set goals for the future. Armaan knows he wants to do his MBA and become the CEO of a multinational corporation one day. Neha wants to become a chartered accountant. Stan has already started DJ-ing at parties. He dreams of becoming the next Hardwell.

And me? Well, I haven't thought that far ahead. All I know is that I have two more years left to complete my BCom degree and I plan on making the most of my college years. I know how stressful the 'real' world is. I've watched my cousins work like dogs; they wish they could travel back in time to when they were in college. So, I'm in no hurry to grow up.

Two hours and four vodka and Cokes later, Neha, Armaan and I are swinging our hips to '*Balam pichkari*'. You've got to love Bollywood night at Copa! Stan is probably chatting with the DJ at his console. I look to my left; Armaan is smiling at Neha, who's standing across from us. She smiles back at him, tucks a strand of her hair behind her ear and looks away coyly. Armaan inches closer to her. Ooh! Something is finally going to happen between these two! I have no idea why I'm so excited! It's probably because my love life is so uneventful. Anyway, just as Neha draws closer to Armaan, someone taps her shoulder. She turns to look at him and I take a few steps to my right so I can see who it is. Fuck. It's Neha's ex, Varun. He has the worst timing ever. He whispers something in Neha's ear and the two of them make their way out of the club. I start towards Neha when Armaan blocks my way.

'What are you doing?' I protest. 'Let me go. She's going to get sucked in by that asshole's bullshit again. You know the effect he has on her.'

'I know. But she's a big girl. She can take care of herself. Remember what happened the last time?'

Varun had interrupted us during dinner at Yauatcha on Neha's birthday a few months ago. Armaan and I had told Varun to leave but Neha asked him to join us instead. Despite the way he had treated her, he had this strange hold on her. She went all goo-goo eyed around him. They thought alike – in the sense they shared the opinion that he was the best thing to have happened to this world. It was extremely frustrating to watch. I can only imagine how Armaan feels now. I pat his back and ask him if he wants another drink. We go to the bar and order a round of Jagermeisters. I really shouldn't drink anymore. I'm beginning to have trouble walking in a straight line but really, what difference will one more drink make at this point?

A few hours later, we're still drinking. Although I've lost track of time, I reckon it must be about 2.00 a.m. The party has now moved to Stan's flat. Neha insisted on bringing Varun along and we had no option but to acquiesce. We would rather bear a few hours with him than lose track of Neha – she would definitely have abandoned us and gone off someplace else with him if we had raised any objections to having him hang out with us.

Stan and I have been dancing for what seems like forever. My feet are beginning to ache. I flop down on the red bean bag in the corner of Stan's living room. Armaan is slouched on the far end of the couch, sipping on his drink. I sidle over on the bean bag to him.

'You okay?' I ask Armaan.

He's staring at Varun, who is whispering into Neha's ear. She giggles exaggeratedly in response.

'Huh? Uh ... yeah ... I'm fine. I guess,' he mumbles.

'I'm sorry, man. I can imagine how pissed off you must be. I mean, *I* want to kill Varun! And I just hate how she behaves when she's with him. It's like she's possessed or something. It's freaky. I can't ever imagine a guy having that effect on me.'

'Ha! No one plans on feeling that way about someone. It just happens. And when it does, you lose control. It may not have happened to you yet, but that doesn't mean it won't happen to you.' Armaan continues staring at Neha and Varun all the while that he's speaking to me. It's like he's talking to himself.

Then he turns to me and says, 'I really hope the guy you fall in love with loves you back, Ti. It's my sincere wish for you. Honestly, I don't want anyone to experience unrequited love. Or like. Or whatever. It really, really sucks. Like I can't tell you how much it sucks. I especially don't want my best friends to go through it.'

Just then, the music playing on my phone is replaced by the sound of my ringtone. Everyone protests as I run to my phone and disconnect it from the speakers.

'Hello?'

'WHERE THE HELL ARE YOU? We have been calling and messaging you for the last two hours! Do you know what time it is?' It's my father and he sounds livid.

'It's around two, I know, Pa. We're all at Stan's place. We'll leave in some time. They'll drop me home, don't worry,' I say.

'It's not two, its five a.m.! This is the limit! When we were nineteen, our curfew was ten p.m.! And why aren't you answering your phone? Have you any idea just how anxious your ma and I have been? You know the kind of things that are happening these days. Do you know how much stress you have put us through...'

With each word my father says I can feel my buzz wearing off. I look at my watch and realize that he has exaggerated only slightly. It's 4.45 a.m. How on earth did I lose track of time like that?

'I'm sorry, Pa. I'm coming home right now. We just didn't realize what time it was.' I quickly hang up. I look helplessly at my friends. 'Guys, my dad is PISSED off. Armaan, can we leave, please?'

'Of course. Let's go,' he says as he rises from the couch.

'Let's have one last drink, na, Ti,' Neha says. When Varun's around, she's oblivious to everyone else.

'It's almost five! My parents are going to kill me. I've got to leave right now. Are you coming with us, Neha?' I ask, making for the door.

'Uh ... you guys go ahead. Varun will drop me,' she replies.

I can see that Armaan is far from happy with this plan. He hesitates for a few seconds and then joins me at the door. We say bye to Stan, Neha and Varun and leave.

The drive home is quiet. It takes only ten minutes from Bandra to JVPD at this time of night (or morning).

'Are you okay?' Armaan asks.

'Huh? I'm fine. I'm a little scared. I've been pushing my luck by coming home late recently. But the latest I've come home is two-thirty. My parents are so angry right now.'

'It will be okay, Ti. Sometimes we think our parents will kick our asses but you'll be surprised by how understanding they can be. Just tell them the truth. You lost track of time and your phone was connected to the speakers. It must have rung when you were out on the balcony so you didn't hear it. Relax. Just apologize to aunty and uncle and it should be okay.'

I nod. I wish I could be as calm as Armaan. I know my parents. They're extremely strict about my curfew and I usually do my best to comply. I guess I just got carried away tonight. I'm such an idiot. Armaan pulls over outside my building. He honks and the security guard walks groggily to open the gate. I walk into the portico, turn around and wave at Armaan. My heart races as I run up the two flights of stairs to my flat. I fumble in my bag for my keys, but before I can put the key in the door, the door is flung open. Pa's face is red. I've never seen him this furious.

'I'm sorry, Pa. Seriously, this won't happen again,' I mutter. I'm waiting for him to yell at me but what happens next leaves me numb.

My father slaps me hard across my face.

'Is this the time decent girls come home? You'll only be happy when you give me a heart attack! No bloody sense of responsibility. Disappearing for hours on end, not taking calls. Do you know the things happening in the city these days? Do you want me to spell it out for you?'

The slap has left me in shock. My cheek is burning. I can feel the humiliation rise within me. A tear slides down my face. Why can't I have normal parents? Why did I have to end up with the most melodramatic set of parents ever? My friends can stay out until the wee hours of the morning without their parents overreacting. Yet I get a slap. That too from my father. What sort of parents hit their teenage daughter? My fear has been replaced by anger. There's nothing left to lose anymore.

'I said I'm sorry. It was a mistake. You don't have to create a scene with the door open so the entire building can hear us. And I'm not a kid anymore. I'm an adult. I know how to take care of myself,' I raise my voice to match my father's.

I can see that I've pushed him over the edge. He grips

my arm and jerks me into the lounge. He slams the door shut. Then he backhands me on my other cheek.

'First, you do something wrong and then you have the nerve to answer back. No manners. No consideration. All you want to do is loaf around and waste your life. Young women from decent families don't come home at five in the morning. Now go to your room before I give you another one.' He raises his arm threateningly.

'Navin, stop it! Tia, go to your room.' The commotion has caused Ma to emerge from the bedroom.

I run to my room. I have no idea when my silent crying turns into sobs. I know I behaved irresponsibly tonight but that doesn't give my father the right to slap me. Violence is never the answer. However, my parents belong to the old school. Their parents hit them when they were kids and so they see nothing wrong in it.

I lie on my bed. The sobbing doesn't stop. I'm crying so hard that I can't breathe through my nose anymore. I hiccup convulsively as I struggle to stop the tears. I haven't cried like this in the longest time. I feel angry, frustrated, humiliated, hurt and trapped. I don't deserve this. My parents don't get me. The gap in our thinking is insurmountable. I simply cannot live like this. I need to get out. I need to get away from this old-fashioned household. I need to go somewhere I can breathe.

APRIL

RACHNA

'So then, Will was all like, "You look really cute today!" And Amy was obviously totally pissed off. And then she walked off. And now she isn't taking my calls. I mean, can you even? Like hello, how is it my fault if your boyfriend is flirting with me, right?' Jo looks expectantly at me for a couple of seconds. That's when I realize she has stopped talking. She wants me to agree with her. How could I forget; Jo constantly needs validation.

'Uh, right. Totally not your fault. But we all know Amy. That's just the way she is. She likes playing the victim. You know she's kind of a drama queen. Why are you even worrying about it? She'll find a new guy she likes in a few weeks and this will all blow over...'

We're sprawled out on Jo's bed. It's just another Saturday afternoon.

'Oh really? Why are you even friends with me if this is what you think about me? Oh wait, maybe I shouldn't react to this. You'll think I'm an even bigger drama queen now! What the eff, Rach? I thought you were my friend!' Amy's voice quavers.

I turn around and find Amy standing in the doorway with a wounded-puppy expression. Fuck. What have I gotten myself into? Me and my stupid, big mouth. I was just trying to comfort Jo. I can feel the blood rush to my cheeks. I jump off the bed and face Amy.

'Amy ... I ... didn't mean that. I was just saying that to comfort Jo ... come on, you know I love you. You're one of my best friends.'

She snorts. 'I'm one of your best friends, but Jo is your absolute BFF. She could murder someone and you would still take her side! That's how it's always been. I don't know why I vent to the two of you. Oh wait, I know why. Because I thought you were my friends. Clearly I was wrong.'

Amy storms out of the room. Jo and I stare at each other in disbelief. Then she says, 'Oh, my God! Can you believe that? Amy really is such a drama queen.'

My jaw drops open. Seriously, Jo? And then I stomp out too.

'Rach! Where are you going? Don't worry, man! Amy's going to come back to us in like two days. It'll be fine.'

I hear Jo call out but I don't stop. I walk out of her house and keep walking until I reach the bus stop, a few blocks down the road.

I perch on the metal seat and stare ahead. It's unseasonably cold (goodbye summer; hello autumn) although the sun is shining. I hate days like this; they're just so misleading. It should either be cold and overcast or sunny and hot. I usually look out of the window and underestimate how cold it is and then realize too late that I should have worn another layer. Anyway, what just happened really bothers me. It's not unlike Jo and Amy to quarrel. In fact, they argue almost every day. But I'm usually the conciliator. This is the first time I got caught in the middle. I know I called Amy a victim and a drama queen to pacify Jo but I truly wish I hadn't used those words. Now that I see it from Amy's perspective, I seem like a back-stabber. But in addition to the remorse, I'm also feeling something else. A strong feeling that I can't quite place. It's like I'm restless but also annoyed. I'm irritated with my friends. I'm sick of their squabbling. I'm sick of these weekends spent at each other's homes watching TV or at the mall. I'm eighteen (I turn nineteen next month, to be accurate) and my life so far has been singularly uneventful. I'm sick of this place. I'm sick and tired of Canberra. This is all I've ever known. Coffee at Ona Coffee. Movies at Dendy. Ice skating at Garema place in winter. Every single year. My life is just so predictable. There's a great big world out there. There *has* to be more to life than being sandwiched between Amy and Jo (not literally – get your mind out of the gutter).

A bus pulls up and I hop in. I sit next to an old lady. She looks at me and smiles.

'Beautiful day, isn't it?'

It really isn't. I've just realized my life sucks. I nod vaguely and smile back.

As the bus trundles through the familiar route to my apartment building, I begin planning my escape from Canberra and the life I've always known. It's time for new beginnings.

MAY

ZAID

'You want to go to study WHERE?' Mum yells.

I sigh. 'I said I want to go to Canada,' I reply calmly.

'And may I ask what's wrong with the university here in Durban?'

'University here is fine. But I can't stand living in Durban anymore. I need to get away. I need to go as far away as possible.'

Mum puts her arms around me. 'I know you want to get as far as possible from Devina, my baby. I know it hurts, son. But running away isn't the solution. It seems impossible to deal with the pain right now but you need to give it some time. You've already come a long way. Trust me, you will get over this.'

'When?' I roar in frustration. 'It's been three months since it ended and my heart still aches every single day. I can't stop thinking about her. Despite everything that she has done to me, I'm still in love with her. What the hell is wrong with me? I have no self-respect. After everything that has happened, I'm still tempted to message or call her. And when I see her on campus, all the old feelings come rushing back. I want to touch her, I want to hear her laugh, I want to talk to her and I also want to scream at her. I want her to feel the way she has made me feel. I want her to be unable to sleep too. I'm ... I'm going mad, Mum.'

Her expression changes. She's beginning to understand just how messed up I am.

'Um ... but how can we ... uh ... afford your education in Canada, Zaid? I'm a single mother. The alimony your father sends barely covers your university fees here. I just ... I just don't know how we can do this. I'm sorry,' she says, resignedly.

'That's okay. I've found a way. I've spoken to the international office on campus. They're affiliated with the University of Guelph in Canada. I can apply to be an exchange student there. I can get a scholarship that covers my flight tickets and I'll get spending money towards my food and accommodation. The fees for the semester will be the same semester fee we've been paying so far – in Rands itself, not in Canadian dollars or anything. And once I'm there, if I find I'm falling short of cash, I can work on campus to support my expenses.'

Mum looks at me incredulously. 'I see you've done your research. You've really thought this through. You're serious,' she says.

'Yes, of course I'm serious. I really need this, Mum. And I need you to say that you're okay with it. I don't want to leave you all by yourself, but I need to do this for myself, Mum, or I will lose my mind. I just have to get away from here. Durban's such a small place that there's no escaping news about Devina. And there's no avoiding running into her either. I need to go to a big city so I can lose myself in the crowd.'

Mum nods. 'Fine. I'll let you go. But only if you promise me one thing.'

'What? What is it? I'll do anything,' I reply.

'Promise me that you'll try to *find* yourself in the crowd.'

I smile at that.

'So, you haven't forgotten how to smile, after all.' She winks.

'I love you, Mum. Thank you.' It looks like I finally have something to look forward to.

JUNE

TIA

I rummage inside my bag for my keys, but the door swings open before I find them. Pa opens the door and looks genuinely surprised to see that I'm back.

'You're home early for once,' Pa says glancing at his watch.

'Hmmm. Yeah ... I couldn't risk another thrashing,' I reply as I shoulder past him to my room.

He looks like he wants to say something but Ma puts her arm around him and stops him.

I shut my bedroom door and flop on my bed. Ever since that night three months ago, I've pulled away from my parents. From the very next day, I started working on my plan to get out of this house. I decided that studying abroad would be the answer. Luckily, we're fairly well off. My father owns a successful jewellery business and my mother helps him run it. I had never considered doing my higher studies outside of Mumbai because I loved my life here. I grew up in Mumbai and I have numerous friends here. I have groups of friends from school, tuition classes, my apartment building and then there's Neha, Stan and Armaan, of course. But everything changed the night Pa slapped me. Not only was it humiliating, I felt wholly demoralized and diminished that day. Like I didn't know what I was doing and couldn't make my own decisions.

But I'm nineteen fucking years old now. I know what I'm doing and I know how to take care of myself. I need my independence. I'm the only nineteen-year-old I know who hasn't ever had a boyfriend. But I can't let life pass me by because of my overprotective parents. The only way I can get to live my life my way is by moving out. And so, I spent the last three months studying for my International English Language Testing System (IELTS) exams. I've turned down oh-so-many party invitations in this time. I was sorely tempted at times to go out just the one time, but I resisted, convincing myself that these sacrifices would pay off in the long run.

On the drive back home today, Armaan asked me what prompted my decision to move to Canada. I wanted to tell him the truth but I couldn't bring myself to do it. It was too mortifying. So I told him a half-truth.

'Oh, I don't know. I just suddenly feel this need to live alone. To be free to make my own decisions. You know how my parents are. I'm just beginning to feel stifled, you know? I'm not a kid anymore. And if I don't do this now, I won't ever get the opportunity to do anything. I worry that I'll just stay on and on and have a predictable, boring life if I don't make this happen now.'

He nodded. 'Wow, I didn't know you feel this way. You've always seemed so happy with your life. But good decision, Ti. I'm sure Canada will be amazing. I'm proud of you for making this happen.'

He smiled at me reassuringly. I felt a surge of confidence. Armaan was right. The future is going to be amazing. I just have to keep the faith.

My reverie is broken by a knock on the door.

'What?' I scream.

'Beta, will you have dinner? There's Thai curry,' Ma says through the door.

'No, I've eaten,' I yell back.

'Okay honey, goodnight.'

'Goodnight,' I mutter grumpily.

Ma has tried to talk to me about what happened a few times. She has asked me to let it go and forgive my father. Even if I am pissed off with Pa, she wants to know why I'm angry with her. Well, of course I'm angry with her. It's her duty as a mother to protect me. When one parent has temper issues, the other needs to be calm and controlled. But both my parents are short-tempered. So, when Pa gets mad at me, Ma just goads him on and vice versa until they're both on a full-fledged rampage. And who do you think suffers in the end? I do. Ma could have stopped Pa from slapping me. She should have intervened sooner.

And as for my father, he never even apologized after what he did. He just carried on like everything was normal. So, I don't care if my father thinks the slaps were justified; I know I won't forgive him, ever.

All I'm doing now is biding my time. I can't wait until it's September and I can get out of here. Canada, here I come.

JULY

FIONA

'I don't understand why we have to break up,' Karan says. The sorrow reflected in his beautiful eyes splinters my heart, but I know I have to do this.

'I love you, baby. You know I do. But I'm going to Canada. And I'm going to study there for four years. How are we supposed to do this?' I ask. I can feel the tears threatening to spill over.

'We'll figure it out, Fi. I love you so much. There's just no way I can love anyone else like this. I'll wait for you. And a long distance relationship can work if you really want to make it work. Plus, you'll come to India during your holidays, right? I don't have the money now, but I'll save up and try and visit you too. Come on, don't do this,' he pleads, taking my hand in his.

Why, oh, why is Karan making this so hard for me? What should I do? I love Karan, I do, but I don't know if he's 'the one'. I mean, I'm nineteen years old, for God's sake. I've hardly lived. I've hardly experienced anything.

Which is why I've worked so hard to make my dream of studying in Canada come true. I want to live and I mean really live. I want to meet new people, I want to travel, I want to have new experiences. And I think those new experiences include dating other people. But clearly, Karan doesn't feel the same way. He's truly, madly and deeply in love with me. I think back to when we first met last year. We met on my first day at Samel Sir's tuition classes. When you study at an all girl's school, tuitions are the only places where one can get to meet boys.

I had gone to Sandhya's place two hours before our tuitions could begin. We had planned our outfits; we wanted to look 'effortlessly good'. We knew that most of the other girls would be wearing shorts and dresses and we didn't want to look like we were trying too hard. So we chose to pair ganjis that highlighted our toned bodies with fitted jeans; casually sexy, see? Sandhya did a side braid for me and I straightened her hair. When we inspected our reflections in the mirror, we liked what we saw. As a result of all the preparations, we reached our tuitions five minutes late and the class was already chock-a-block. We couldn't find seats together, so I sank into a space in the fourth row and Sandhya found a place in the back of the class. I looked to my left and I saw a cute guy listening with rapt attention to Samel Sir and frantically making notes. I didn't even realize I had begun to smile. He turned suddenly and caught me staring at him. I quickly looked away but not before Samel Sir saw us having our moment.

Samel Sir cleared his throat and said in his thick

Indian accent, 'I hope you all know you are here to get better at physics and chemistry – and not waste your parents' hard-earned money on *personal chemistry* with your fellow students. So all the "*lovarr*" (lover) boys and "*gulls*" (girls), stop getting excited that you are sitting next to "*peepul*" (people) of the opposite sex and focus on the class, okay?' He looked directly at Karan and me as he said the last part and I could feel myself blushing furiously as the students around me giggled. After class, I hurriedly packed my books in my bag and got up to join Sandhya, when Karan tapped me on the shoulder.

'Hey, you're forgetting this,' he handed me my notebook.

'Oh! Thank you! God, I'm always leaving my stuff everywhere,' I replied, blushing.

'You're welcome. I'm Karan, by the way. And you are?'

'Fiona. Nice to meet you,' I responded.

Just then Sandhya walked up to us.

'Hey Fi. Your mom just called. Why aren't you answering your phone? She said everyone's waiting for you for dinner.'

'Oh! Okay, got to rush. Bye!' I smiled at Karan as I walked off with Sandhya.

After dinner, I opened my notebook to check my notes from the class when I spotted something written on the inner flap of the book.

Hi! I study at St. Martins and live in GK ... would love to get to know you ... looking forward to seeing you in class on Friday. I'll be here at 4.30. I hope you can come early too? – Karan.

I re-read the message at least a dozen times before calling Sandhya to discuss the very exciting events of the day.

'Oh my God! You're going to have a boyfriend! I can't believe you met someone on your very first day in class! What luck, man! He's so cute. And meanwhile I sat next to a super ugly guy who was stinking!'

I spent the next two days anticipating our meeting on Friday. I loved how we were going about this the old-school way. Karan hadn't given me his number and so there was nothing to do except wait. I reached the class at 4.30 on the dot on Friday only to find Karan sitting on a bench outside the classroom. He broke into a huge smile when he saw me. I smiled coyly at him. We chatted for half an hour before the class could begin and discovered that we had a lot in common. We exchanged numbers this time around and spent the next few days constantly texting each other. I couldn't wait to see him at tuitions. Soon we started meeting on other days as well. And before I knew it, I had a boyfriend.

The year had just whizzed by. And now I was leaving for Canada in a month. I looked at Karan again and nodded slowly.

'Okay. We won't break up. We'll stay in a relationship. But let's promise each other, baby, if either of us meets someone else or feels like this isn't working anymore, we'll be honest and tell the other. No hard feelings. Agreed?' I asked.

He looked at me gratefully and smiled. 'Agreed.'

AUGUST

RACHNA

'I got Cooper Lodge! What did you get?' Jo asks Amy.

'Oh my God! I got Cooper Lodge too! I'm in apartment 501. You?' Amy asks excitedly.

'No way! I'm in 505! I can't believe it! This is awesome! We're going to have so much fun! I'm so glad we're going to be together, Amsicle!' Jo claps. Amy leaps out of bed and rushes to the study desk where Jo is poring over her letter. The two of them hug, oblivious to my dumbfounded expression.

When Amy and Jo realized that I wouldn't be going to university in Australia, they made sure they attended the same university so at least they could be together. And they've become super close over the last few months. In the past, they found it hard to hang out without me acting as a buffer to keep them from biting each other's heads off. But now it looks like they're going to manage perfectly well without me.

I can't help but feel a pang. I don't know what I

expected. Obviously I knew that everyone's lives wouldn't stop once I left, but I'm feeling vulnerable nonetheless. Amy and Jo have been increasingly behaving like they don't need me anymore. And I can't help wondering if I've made a wise decision by giving up the familiarity of studying at home and choosing to venture off into the unknown. What if I don't make any friends in college?

I leave Amy's place and walk home. I live just a block away from Amy and because I'm so lost in my thoughts, I reach home even quicker than usual today.

My older sister, Aisha, opens the door when I knock.

'Rach, don't you think it sucks that we don't have a family song?' she asks seriously, when I enter the house.

'What?'

'I'm watching *Yaadon ki Baarat*. It struck me that we don't have a family song. What if we all lose each other like they did in the movie?'

'Um, they were kids when they were separated which is why they needed a family song to recognize each other by when they grew up. In case you haven't noticed, we're already grown up. Why am I even replying to this? You talk so much crap, Aish.'

'Whatever. A family song is fun. We can sing it at each other's weddings. We should pick a song we all like. And it should be festive. How about '*Maahi ve*' from *Kal Ho Na Ho*?'

'Whatever. Pick whatever you want. Where's Mama?'

'In her room. Doing yoga.'

I head to Mama's room. The door is ajar. Her body is contorted in a complicated asan.

'Mama?'

She waves at me. 'Hi, honey. Want to join me?'

'No. I don't feel like it. I wanted to ask you something, Mama.'

She untangles herself from her pose and sits cross-legged on her mat. She pats the bean bag next to her, motioning me to sit.

I flop onto the bean bag and then begin. 'Mama, do you think I'm doing the right thing by going to Canada to study?'

'Of course, Rach. Why? What's wrong? You were excited all this while. What happened now?'

'I don't know. Amy and Jo are going to uni together. Right here in Canberra. And I suddenly realized I don't know anyone in Canada. Amy and Jo bug me sometimes but they've become like family. What if I don't find friends like that again? What if no one likes me there? And you guys won't be around either. I'm going to be so alone!'

Mama reaches out and takes my hand in hers. 'First things first, take a deep breath. You'll immediately feel better.' She waits until I inhale and exhale.

'Feeling better? Now listen, beta, we all come into this world alone. And we're all going to leave alone too. A human being is very strong. We can all survive in the direst of circumstances. And how will you know what you're capable of until you've tested your limits? The Bhagvadgita says that whatever is happening, is happening for the good; whatever will happen, will also happen for the good. You need not worry about the future. What is yours today, belonged to someone else yesterday, and will belong to someone else the day after tomorrow.'

I sigh. 'I don't want to know about the Bhagvadgita again, Mama. I just want to know if I'm going to be okay.'

'If you decide to be okay, you'll be okay,' Mama says sagely. When she looks at my exasperated expression, she rises and engulfs me in a bear hug.

'Why are you getting stressed out, beta? Everything will be okay. I promise. I'm proud of you for deciding to do something different. Follow your heart and it will not lead you astray.'

'But won't you miss me?'

'Of course, I will. More than you can imagine. But you're growing up. It's time for you to fly out of the nest. And you know I would never clip your wings.'

I smile. Trust Mama to put everything in perspective. No wonder all her yoga students always come out of class smiling. I think about all the times during my school days when I wept and told her that I was afraid I would fail my exams. And each time she would ask me to imagine a bright light entering my mind and assure me that everything would be fine. She would insist that the most important thing was that I had done my karma by studying. The sceptic in me always wondered how much her reiki, pranic healing and yoga really helped, but I couldn't deny that I felt better after spending time with Mama. And I couldn't deny that she definitely had a calming aura. Mama's face glowed with wisdom. I had to admire how calm she always was. Aisha, the crazy one in our family, was constantly doing outlandish things – like insisting on keeping a pet hamster, which was allowed to roam at large about the house when she was ten; literally giving the clothes off her back to a homeless person (she came home in just her bra and jeans because she felt that a homeless lady needed her jersey more than she did); or the time she pierced her tongue, eyebrows and nose, and got a tattoo, all on the same day, when she was fifteen; or more recently, dropping out of college to start her own jewellery-making business (the jewellery is hideous).

Any other mother would have lost her patience with Aisha (I mean, *I* wanted to kill her more times a week than I cared to count) but Mama embraced Aisha's quirks wholly and unconditionally. Although Papa often accused Mama of encouraging Aisha, she knew that hindering Aisha would cause her to rebel and get even crazier (if that were possible).

In comparison, I was always the studious, sane one. Which is why choosing to study abroad is so out of character for me. But just because I'm not as eccentric as Aisha, it doesn't mean I can't have some adventures of my own.

It's going to be okay, I tell myself. The best is yet to come.

PART 2

SEPTEMBER

She felt cold even before she stepped through the glass doors. 'This is it. I'm actually here. I'm in Toronto.' Tia let it sink in.

She walked over to the airport shuttle and managed to hoist her heavy suitcase from the trolley and stow it in the luggage compartment at the bottom of the bus. She was surprised to note that there were no attendants to help passengers with their luggage. Back home, there were attendants for everything. She boarded the crowded shuttle and managed to find a window seat at the rear of the bus. Google had informed her that the drive from the airport to her university would take an hour. She jammed the earphone plugs into her ears and plugged the jack into her phone before gazing out of the window.

She reached campus and gaped at the impressive edifices in front of her. The first building that greeted her was the University Centre or UC – a simple grey building surrounded by towering trees. She walked along the pathway within the expansive campus gazing at the impressive university buildings and magnificent gardens.

She stopped at Johnston Hall. It was a grey-bricked building with creepers adorning the walls. The clock on the main tower of the building made it the university's best-known landmark. It was beautiful. Johnston Hall faced a huge garden. Man, the campus was humungous! It was so different from the single building that was her 'campus' back home. Home. She should probably give her mother a call. She must be getting stressed out. But how would she call her? She needed to get a calling card for that. However, there was so much more to do first. She would have to get her room keys from the administrator in her residence building. Then visit the International Students Office to find out what her next steps should be. She knew that there was a mixer for international students that evening, which was why she had chosen to arrive three days before college officially started. She wanted to receive the proper orientation for international students and 'settle in' before her first day at college. But she was already exhausted. Her legs were hurting from the endless walking. Where was this godforsaken res building?

Just then, she spotted a twelve-storey brownstone building a few metres away. Although she had seen the image on her laptop way too many times, seeing it live was something else. This would be her new home. She quickened her pace to the building.

She made her way through the entrance of the building and located the administrator's desk.

'Hi there,' the admin lady greeted her. She had a bright smile that calmed Tia down.

'Hi, I'm moving in today. I'm from India. I got here

early for the International Students' Mixer,' she replied.

'Oh, wow! How exciting! I've always wanted to go to India. You have to tell me all about it. I'm Jane by the way. But wait, did you land in Canada just today?'

'Yup. Got off the plane, took the shuttle, and here I am.'

'You must be exhausted, you poor thing! So you received an email with your apartment number assigned to you, right?'

Tia dug out the printed email from her handbag. 'Flat 604, level six,' she read from it.

Jane typed the information in and peered at her computer. She nodded. She bent down and emerged with the keys.

'It's a set of two keys. This one's for the main door and this is your room key,' she said pointing the two out to Tia. 'Now remember, campus is quite safe but you've got to take care of your things. Lock your room when you're out. You may trust your roomies, but you never know, right?'

Tia smiled. Jane had a warm maternal vibe.

'Yes, thanks, Jane. I'll see you around.'

She dragged her bag and took the elevator up to the sixth floor. She let herself into her apartment and found herself in a lounge area furnished with comfortable chairs. The kitchen was to her right. She carefully navigated her suitcase past the furniture to her bedroom door. She turned the key to reveal a room with a single bed, a cupboard, a desk and a chair with a large window above the desk. This was her room. Never mind that her room back home was three times the size of this room. This was her very own space. Her parents wouldn't be around to monitor her every move. She took a deep breath. She was free at last.

Rachna woke up with a start. She was in a strange bed in a strange room. What was happening? It took her a few minutes of staring at the ceiling to realize where she was. And just as she was about to close her eyes again, it hit her. She was supposed to attend the International Students' Mixer! She looked at her watch. It was 3.00 a.m. Huh? Oh, wait. She hadn't reset her watch yet. She quickly worked out the time in her head. It was 5.30 in the evening. Shit! The mixer started an hour ago. She had planned on dressing with care for the event but she couldn't risk missing it altogether. She wore a jersey over her T-shirt and jeans. She applied some kajal and gloss and brushed her hair. The frizzy hair at the top of her head refused to settle down and as a result, she looked like she had just been electrocuted. After attempting to flatten it for a few seconds, she gave up. She locked her room and made her way to Rozanski Hall. She had glimpsed the building when she had arrived from the airport earlier that day, so she knew it was a five-minute walk.

When she reached the venue, she pushed the door open. The room wasn't as full as she'd expected. There were just about forty people or so. Surely, the university had more international students than that?

A bald man in his fifties who looked like he was in the middle of addressing the room, looked at her enquiringly.

'Hi, uh. Sorry I'm late. I didn't mean to disrupt your talk.' She looked at him as she spoke, but was loud enough for the entire room to hear her.

'Relax. Welcome. We were just having an informal chat. I'm Jeff White. I'm the International Student Advisor. I was just telling everyone that I'm available to chat whenever you're confused about something. Grab a kit from that table, would you? It's a very helpful kit. Or so I'd like to believe. But seriously, you'll find information on meal plans, frequently asked questions and a campus map among other things.'

She picked up a colourful folder from the table and sat down next to a pretty Chinese girl.

'So finally, I need you all to remember that I'm in room 304 in the UC if you ever need to talk. And remember, you're here to study but you're also here to have a good time! So make lots of friends, join campus clubs and participate in as many activities as you can. One last thing; don't be gullible, okay? You *have* to look out for yourself now. Make good decisions, guys. For example, don't lend money to a "friend" you've just met. Make sure that they're not taking advantage of you because they know some of you are exchange students here for just the semester. They may "borrow" money from you that you may never see again!' He paused while some of the students chuckled at this. Rachna found herself smiling. Then he looked straight at Rachna and said, 'And all you young ladies, don't fall for the bad boys, okay? Take care of yourselves.'

Rachna wondered why he addressed that solely to her. Did she look gullible?

'Okay, that's it. I'm not going to lecture you anymore. This is a mixer so please mingle and make some friends.'

The room erupted in chatter as people started getting up and talking to each other. Rachna wondered who she should talk to. The Chinese girl had risen from her seat before Rachna could initiate a conversation. She already seemed to know a bunch of people and was chattering away with a group of five Chinese students. Rachna was looking around for someone to talk to when she spotted him.

The first thing that she noticed about him was that he was Indian. Now she wasn't racist or anything, but she couldn't help but feel excited to see another Indian student. He was tall-ish (around 5'11"?) and looked about as tall as Will, Amy's boyfriend. What caught her eye first was the deep cleft in his chin, which was visible through his scruffy beard. His hair was rather messy, too. She was happy to note that she wasn't the only one who hadn't brushed her hair here. His jaw was definitely his strongest feature. He had light brown eyes, a flat nose and full lips. He wasn't the most attractive guy she had ever met, but there was definitely something about him. He met her eye and she felt the blood rush to her cheeks. Instinctively she looked away. Oh, God! He must think she was checking him out (which she kinda was, but why should he know that?). She glanced at him again and this time smiled confidently. She expected him to return her smile, but all she got was a blank look. Although slightly taken aback, she decided to talk to him anyway.

'Hi, I'm Rachna. And you are?'

'Zaid,' he replied.

He's definitely not from India, she thought, trying to place his accent. She realized she wasn't going to get any more from, him, so she continued, 'So, where are you from Zaid?'

'Durban, South Africa.'

'Oh, wow! I've always wanted to go to South Africa. It's on my must-see list. I'm from Australia. Well, originally from Bangalore, India, but my family moved to Australia when I was a kid.' She realized he hadn't exactly asked her where she was from, but rambled on anyway. When he didn't say anything, she prodded.

'So, uh, have you ever been to Australia?'

'No. Born and brought up in South Africa. This is my first time out of S.A. actually.'

Woah! He had never been out of his country? Rachna remembered how much she had carped and complained when she hadn't been able to get out of Canberra for a holiday one year. And that was *one* year! How on earth had Zaid managed to live in one place for eighteen or nineteen years and not wanted to get out until now? She had so many questions but he appeared taciturn and aloof. He kept glancing around with this vacant look on his face; far from the excitement and nervousness evident on all the other students' faces. It seemed like he just didn't want to be there. Or maybe he just didn't want to be there with *her*. Maybe her crazy hair and overall scruffiness had put him off (he wasn't the most well-put-together guy either, but then again guys could be pretty judgemental). Finally giving up, she excused herself and walked further ahead.

She was wondering who to talk to when a girl walked up to her.

'Hi! I'm Precious. And you?'

'I'd like to believe I'm precious, too!' Rachna replied.

The girl laughed. 'I'm sure you are! I'll rephrase that. My name's Precious and I'm from Nigeria.' Precious smiled a big smile at her and Rachna found herself smiling back. At last! Someone wanted to be friends with her! She spent the next half hour deep in conversation with Precious. It turned out that Precious's res. building was on the other side of campus. She was studying Business Administration, which was completely different from Rachna's Engineering degree and that meant that they wouldn't have any classes together. But Rachna hit it off with her. Conversation flowed with Precious and after talking to her for just half an hour, Rachna knew she had made a friend. She had always wondered why some people clicked immediately while others spent lifetimes never understanding each other. The comfortable vibe which was completely missing when she spoke with Zaid was a hundred per cent present with Precious. She looked around her to see what he was up to. She really wanted to know if he was standoffish in general or only with her. She found him sipping a drink in the far corner of the room. It didn't seem like he was interested in talking to anyone at the mixer. How odd. Rachna turned back to her new friend and continued her conversation. She had felt lonely when she first arrived at the campus, but now she was beginning to feel it would be alright after all.

Zaid stood back and surveyed his handiwork. He had painted stars, a moon and the word 'Hope'. The 'Art Walk' was the only event that had interested him in the day's orientation activities. Everything else involved 'mingling'; something he couldn't stand to do. He was surprised at what he had painted. Who knew he still had hope left in him? He'd picked up a paintbrush for the first time in what, seven years now? He'd forgotten how therapeutic painting could be. He'd been pretty good at art when he was a kid. And then when he became a teenager, painting seemed 'girly' to him. So he started spending his time playing games on his X box instead.

'Good job, you guys! I love this! We're going to display this at the entrance of Glengarry and it's going to stay up for the entire year. 2016 is going to be the best!' an enthusiastic Resident Advisor said to the group of twenty-odd students who had been painting the mural for the last hour.

'Help yourself to some cookies and cupcakes. Welcome to Glengarry! Talk to each other, guys! You're all res. mates,' the Resident Advisor continued. Zaid took that as his cue to leave as people in the group began talking to each other. He walked to the table laden with goodies and picked up a red velvet cupcake. He bit into it and started walking aimlessly.

He read from the activity guide for the day. Speed-dating at 4.00 p.m. No thanks. Karaoke at 5.00 p.m.

Hell, no! Mingle over a barbeque? Mingle over ice-cream? Prayer walk? Zaid sighed. Orientation week was proving to be stressful. The week was all about familiarizing new students with the university. Every day for a week, there were loads of 'fun' social activities planned. Every activity Zaid attended so far, had inevitably involved interacting with groups of people. Although Zaid had only attended the activities for the free food, he had been compelled to 'participate' and try to make friends. He wasn't sure how much longer he could do this. Fortunately, it was the last day of Orientation Week. An activity captioned on the board caught his eye: 'Watch the *Blind Side* at Prairie Hall at 4.30 p.m.'

He loved that movie! He had always been a sucker for movies about underdogs. And he loved sports movies. This movie was the perfect amalgamation of his favourite genres of films. Finally! An activity worthy of his time. He checked his watch. It was 4.40 p.m. Shit! He needed to reach Prairie Hall as soon as possible. He quickened his pace but his progress was impeded by the thronging students who were merrily mingling and hanging out at the stalls.

Man, I hope I get a place to sit, he thought as he entered the hall of the res., five minutes later. The hall had a grand total of ten students! What? You've got to be kidding me. Did people actually choose speed-dating and karaoke over an amazing movie? What was wrong with everyone?

As he made his way to a seat at the back of the room, he spotted a counter with popcorn. Sweet! An Orientation

Week volunteer behind the counter handed him a large tub of popcorn. 'Enjoy the movie.' She smiled at him.

He found himself smiling back at her. His favourite movie *and* free popcorn. He had to admit Orientation Week wasn't that stupid after all.

He was engrossed in the movie; Sandra Bullock's character, Leanne, had just invited Big Mike, to stay the night at her place. That was when he was distracted by a loud cackle from the row behind him. Two girls were giggling and chatting incessantly. He wanted to turn around and ask them to pipe down but decided to wait for a bit to see if they would shut up on their own. When their jabbering wouldn't let up, he felt he just couldn't take it anymore. He twisted around in his seat and said, 'Can you please keep it down? Some of us are trying to watch the movie.'

The girls looked startled. He recognized one of them; it was the girl he had seen at the International Students' Mixer. The chatty girl from Australia. Her name began with an 'R', he knew that much.

She looked pissed off and retorted, 'Why don't you lighten up? This isn't class. We're allowed to talk. And if we're bothering you so much, you're welcome to find another seat.'

He decided to let it go. He had been an ass to her at the mixer and that was probably why she was prickly towards him now. Under normal circumstances, he would have reciprocated her friendliness at the mixer and she wouldn't have hated his guts. But if things were normal, he wouldn't even really be in Canada. He would still have been in Durban, happy to be dating the girl of his dreams.

There it was again. Ever since he had broken up with Devina, he had inevitably thought about her every single day. Some days, he would make it until bedtime without having had a single thought about her, but then, the minute he got into bed, he would find his mind wandering back to her again. There was simply no escaping her. He sighed. He had missed precious minutes of his favourite film thanks to Devi. He tried to concentrate on the movie but he couldn't get himself to enjoy it. He felt empty. He looked around him; the other people watching the movie were cheerful. In fact, everyone on campus looked so excited. And why shouldn't they? They were young; they had the rest of their lives ahead of them. He was young too; he knew that. But he simply had nothing to look forward to. He had thought that starting afresh in a new country would do the trick. He was realizing now that changing your surroundings is easy; it's changing what's happening on the inside that's tough.

'Does this skirt make my butt look big?' Natalie asked Fiona.

Natalie was 5'7" and weighed fifty kilos. She was drop-dead gorgeous.

'Of course not, Nat. Your butt looks perfect. My stomach looks really bad in this dress, though. I'm changing,' Fiona replied. Fiona knew she was pretty; she wasn't being conceited, just honest. At 5'5" and fifty-three kilos, Fiona was slender. She'd been blessed with porcelain skin and soft, long locks. Her close-set eyes, sharp nose and thick lips resulted in an appealing combination. But Natalie was a blue-eyed, blonde with a smile to die for and legs that went on for ages. And when they stood together, Natalie simply was more striking.

'No way! You look amazing. Like an Indian Goddess!'

Fiona giggled. 'Have you smoked up already? I thought we were going to smoke up together!'

'I waited for you to get back from class, but Arjun came by so we shared a joint. But, no worries, I have two right here. So hurry up and get dressed. We have twenty minutes until the cab arrives.'

Fiona felt a pang. Why couldn't she have been around when Arjun came over? Why was she jealous that Nat and Arjun hung out? She had a boyfriend back home who loved her a lot. She had no business falling for someone else.

She thought back to the first time she met Arjun. It was during Orientation Week. Fiona shared an apartment suite on campus with five girls – Natalie, Candice, Emma, Laura and Claire. Laura and Claire had struck up a friendship as soon as they had met. They kept to themselves and didn't seem to want to hang out with the rest. Candice and Emma were alright but seemed to already have friends on campus and didn't seem very keen on becoming besties with Fiona. Natalie had moved in two days after the official 'move in' day. She had greeted Fiona enthusiastically when she entered the flat. It turned out that they shared two classes in addition to their taste in music and movies. And when you're in college, that's more than enough in common to build a solid friendship. Natalie was outgoing and had the Canadian 'super-friendly gene'. She could strike up a conversation with anyone and everyone. This skill, combined with her looks, made her extremely popular within a week of being on campus.

Every time Fiona walked with Nat on campus, they would bump into at least a dozen people who knew Natalie. Fiona generally smiled politely at whatever new friend Nat introduced her to and didn't think much of anyone she met. She was content being Nat's sidekick. But when she met Arjun, something inside her stirred. It was the last day of Orientation, and Nat had persuaded Fiona to attend a speed-dating session. Fiona wasn't interested in meeting any guys; she intended on staying loyal to Karan. Although she had never attended a speed-dating session and had only ever seen these in American TV shows and movies, she was always intrigued by them. So, she accompanied Nat to the one-hour session. Time flew by; she spoke to various guys for the stipulated ten minutes each. Most of the guys were pretty average, one of the guys was very funny and she could see herself being friends with him. She had enjoyed herself and was midway through the session when he sat down in front of her. And for the first time that afternoon, she found herself tongue-tied. He looked like a Greek god and she wasn't even exaggerating. He was six feet tall, had blue-green eyes and really sharp features. Damn, boy! He looked like a friggin' super model!

'Hi, I'm Arjun. I'm from Japan. Well, I'm originally

from the US, but I've spent most of my life in Japan. I was born in California but we moved around the world, thanks to my dad's job. And you?' he said in a distinctly American accent.

'I … um … I'm Fiona. I'm from India. Born and brought up there. Are you Indian? You don't really look Indian,' she blurted the last bit without really thinking.

He laughed. 'Well, my dad's Indian and my mum's American.' He looked right into her eyes and smiled at her. 'So enough of the generic stuff. Ten minutes is not usually enough to really get to know someone but I would like to give it a shot. Tell me something you don't usually share with strangers.' He continued staring at her and she found her heart skipping a beat. What was happening to her? No guy had ever had this effect on her before. Not even Karan. Oh, my God, Karan. Surely flirting with other people also classified as cheating? She had to answer Arjun though; he continued to look at her expectantly.

'Well, I … I fantasize that I'm a race car driver sometimes. Like a really cool, powerful woman who wears this bodysuit and isn't afraid of anything. Kind of like that scene from *Charlie's Angels*, you know what I mean? But I guess it's going to remain a fantasy because I'm terrified of driving! I failed my driver's test in India. And this is after paying my instructor to ensure I get a license. You know, they give licenses to anybody and everybody in India. The idiots on the Indian roads are proof of that. But me, *I* couldn't get one!' Her cheeks grew warm. This wasn't the smartest thing to say. She should have told him something else; something that portrayed her as mysterious and sexy. Nowhere in Cosmo's tips on attracting men had she read: 'tell him your weaknesses and fears.' She didn't want him to think she was a damsel-in-distress. But the damage had been done. He was about to reply when the buzzer went off, indicating that their time was up.

He smiled at her and said, 'It has been a pleasure getting to know you, Fiona. Let's talk after the session?' He rose and sat on the chair diagonal to her. It was his turn to get to know Nat now. She tried to concentrate on the guy in front of her but she kept hearing snippets of Arjun's conversation with Nat. 'Wow, your biceps are huge! I've been trying to build muscle for the last few months and I've been doing weights for a while now. You want to feel? My biceps, I mean.' Nat giggled.

God! She is so good at flirting. How is Arjun going to resist that?

'What classes are you taking?' the guy seated in front of her asked.

'Huh? Oh, I'm doing Engineering and Design, Programming, Chemistry and Calculus,' Fiona replied distractedly.

He asked her another question and she forced herself to try and pay attention to him. She couldn't even remember his name and he had introduced himself just five minutes ago. It was either Ryan or Bryan. Although there were just five minutes to go before the end of this 'speed-date', it felt like forever.

The buzzer finally went off and she heaved a sigh of relief.

'Okay guys, we're almost at the end of the session. You have two more speed dates to go. We hope you've enjoyed yourself and made some friends if not met some potential partners!' the organizer of the event announced.

The last two dates went by in a blur; the guys didn't seem very interested in Fiona either and so no hearts were broken. When the session ended, Nat came up to Fiona excitedly. 'So, wasn't this fun? I gave my number to like five of these guys. As for the rest, I was like, hell no!'

As they walked out of the room, Arjun came up to them.

'So, the two prettiest girls here know each other,' he said.

Fiona blushed.

'We don't just know each other, we're roomies too!' Nat said.

'Oh awesome! You said you stay in Lanark, right? I'm in Dundee. We're super close. I'm going to see a lot of you two, I hope.' He smiled.

'For sure! What's your number?' Nat asked.

They exchanged numbers and even though Arjun looked at both of them while he spoke, Fiona couldn't help but feel like a third wheel. Nat was at her flirtatious best and Arjun was clearly charmed by her. It bugged Fiona that Nat simply assumed that Fiona wasn't interested in Arjun. 'But you told her about Karan. You told her you were in a happy relationship,' her mind reasoned. 'But that was before I met an interesting, gorgeous half-Indian guy who grew up in Japan!' What struck her about Arjun was that he was smart in addition to being good looking.

Fiona had always been attracted to intelligent guys who were good conversationalists.

It had been two weeks since that first meeting. Arjun, Nat and Fiona had hung out quite a bit since they met. He had come over to their flat to watch a movie. They had all gone downtown for dinner. They had attended parties on campus together. And every time she met him, Fiona felt her crush intensify. In the past, Fiona had found it really easy to determine whether someone had a crush on her, but, with Arjun, it was really hard to tell. At times, she felt certain that there was something between them; at others, she felt like she was imagining it. Arjun stared intently at whoever he was conversing with, so the if-he-stares-into-your-eyes-he-likes-you theory couldn't be applied to him. Fiona had also tried to determine whether Nat liked him; but she seemed pretty non-committal as well.

'We're young. I don't want to get tied down. I just want to have fun right now,' Nat had said when she had asked her about Arjun.

What Nat classified as 'having fun' was a mystery, however. Did sleeping with Arjun classify as having fun? Or would she restrict herself to merely flirting with him? It was all very vague. Meanwhile, Karan called Fiona every day. He would tell her how much he missed her and she would reply saying that she missed him too. Although, truth be told, her new life had engulfed her completely. Between classes, assignments and socializing, she didn't have time to miss Karan. Heck, she hardly even watched TV anymore. She was so busy living her life; she didn't have time to watch other people living it up on TV.

'Fi fi! Smoke up,' Nat interrupted her thoughts, offering her a joint.

Fiona took a drag and exhaled. She felt herself relax with every drag she took and by the time the cab came, she was giggling uncontrollably. She was ready to party. Nat was right; they were young, gorgeous and free! What more could they ask for? God, she loved her life right now.

'Please do your dishes. The sink is overflowing with them. Thanks, Stephanie.' Tia read the note stuck on her room door and sighed as she entered her room. She listlessly dropped her bag on the floor and climbed into bed. She was exhausted. Her day had started at 7.00 a.m. She had had back-to-back classes until noon. Then, she had to work on two assignments, which were due the next day. After spending five hours in the library working on the assignments, she had to go to work at the alumni centre where she had taken up a post as a part-time call-centre representative. All she wanted to do now was sleep. The note from her anal roommate was the final straw. Tia had tried to stay strong for the last few weeks, but the stress finally got to her. She gave in to her tears. She heard her phone ring and saw that it was a Facetime call from Armaan. It was surprising to hear from him. He was the type of friend who was bad at keeping in touch, but when you eventually did meet up, it would be like nothing had changed.

She considered ignoring it. She hated crying in front of people, even if they were her friends. But she was also feeling extremely lonely. It would be good to see a familiar face. She answered it and he appeared on her screen.

'Ti! How have you been, man? You've totally forgotten us. You must be having so much fun!' he said enthusiastically.

'Um ... well, I've had a pathetic day actually,' Tia replied, sniffling.

'Shit. Are you crying? What's wrong, Ti?' he asked gently.

'I'm just ... I don't know! Everything is so hard! I'm just tired. I've got to do everything by myself. I have to fix my breakfast, do the laundry and the dishes. And we have tons of assignments due all the time. And I'm also doing a part-time job! It's just too much! And I've typed a whole lot of crap for one of my assignments due tomorrow. I think I'm going to fail!' she wailed.

'You're not going to fail, Ti. Come on! You're smart. I understand that living alone and doing everything yourself can be overwhelming and exhausting. But you also get to learn how strong you are when you're put in situations like these, right? I'm really proud of you for making all this happen. You dove into the unknown. You could have easily chosen what was comfortable and stayed home in Bombay. But you picked the harder path. And that takes guts,' Armaan said.

She took a deep breath. 'You really think I'm brave?' she asked.

'Of course! And I also know for a fact that you're going to have a great time there. It has only been three weeks. The first few weeks in a new place are always the hardest. Then you settle in and make new friends. Just give it more time, you're going to love it there, I'm sure of that. You're not going to want to leave.'

She smiled at him. 'Thanks, Armaan. I really needed some reassurance. Sorry for breaking down like that. You must be wondering what hit you.'

'Shut up. You don't need to thank me. What are friends for? I'm here whenever you need to talk, okay?'

'Okay! So, anyway, enough about me. How are things there? How's the gang doing? Do you fools miss me or not?'

'Of course not! Why would we miss you? We have better things to do with our time. I'm joking, come on! Of course, we miss you. Everyone is good. Nothing has really changed here. Same old, same old. Oh actually, one thing has changed. Or actually has it? It's the same story over and over again and we all know how it ends,' Armaan said.

'What? What are you saying?'

'Neha and Varun are back together. Surprise, surprise!' He tried to sound nonchalant, but she heard the bitterness in his voice and almost saw the despair in his eyes.

'No way! Why? Why does Neha not see what a douche Varun is? I'm sorry, Armaan,' Tia said. No wonder Armaan had called her; he needed someone to talk to.

'Sorry for what, Ti? I care about her, so I hate seeing the effect he has on her. But I've come to realize that she is responsible for her own actions. We all know that she is going to get her heart broken again, but there really is nothing we can do about it.' He sighed.

'Yeah, I find it super frustrating too. But I know it

affects you more. Why don't you just tell her how you feel? There is chemistry between you two; everyone sees that. Just show her what it would be like to date a nice guy and she'll never go back to that asshole.'

He nods. 'Maybe you're right. Sorry, I'm dumping all my crap on you when you have so much going on.'

'Shut up, Armaan. You know you can talk to me whenever you want. It is actually good to hear about your problems; it makes me feel like I'm not the only one going through shit,' she said.

He laughed. 'Gee, thanks! I'm glad my problems make you feel better.'

'Anytime.' She laughed too.

Thank God Armaan had called when she needed to talk to someone. She felt much better than she had a few minutes ago.

'Okay, I've got to go and clear out the sink before my bitchy roommate kills me! Bye, A! We should do this more often,' she said.

'Bye, Ti! Done! Let's make this a weekly thing. I'll call you next Wednesday. Make sure you have stories for me. Take care and don't work so hard. Go clubbing on Saturday, okay? And meet some cute *gora* boys. You have all the freedom in the world, *beta*! No mama-papa calling you every five minutes! Please make the most of it.'

As she did her dishes, she thought about what Armaan had said. She really did need to unwind. She had to make her weekend count. She was going to have to find a way to have fun amidst all the work. Huh! Who knew Armaan could be so wise?

Zaid looked at his assignment and smiled. Eighty-five per cent was awesome! He had really worked hard and it was good to see his hard work pay off. He collected his assignment from Professor Gatewood and walked out of class. He had nothing due on Monday, which meant he could catch up on his sleep this weekend.

He was just about to enter his res. when he heard someone call his name. He turned around and saw a guy approach him. Where did he know him from? Oh right, Marketing. He was the guy who never showed up at their assignment group meetings.

'Hey, bro! Fab job on the assignment. I just found out that it counts for twenty-five per cent of our semester marks. That is brilliant!' he replied.

Zaid nodded. 'Yeah, it is pretty cool. I'm sorry, I've forgotten your name.'

'No worries, bro. I'm Arjun. Listen, I know that girl, Dana, totally wanted to complain about me to Prof. Gatewood and didn't want me to get the same marks as you guys since I didn't do any of the work. I heard that you were against the idea of complaining though, so I really owe you one.'

'Yeah well, it just felt like a very high-school thing to do; complain about your classmate. But why didn't you show up for at least one meeting?'

Arjun looked sheepish. 'Well, I … kinda had a rough week. I was totally going to make it to that last meeting but then I kinda got stoned.'

Zaid was not amused. He knew a lot of people smoked up on campus but he had never tried weed and didn't intend on trying it either. A friend of his had overdosed on cocaine when he was in high school and died. The incident had put Zaid off drugs completely. He just felt like it was such a waste of a life. Mo had been talented and smart. He had had his whole life ahead of him and had lost it all for a temporary high. He knew weed was mild and if done sparingly, pretty harmless too, but he just didn't believe in indulging in drugs.

'Well, I wouldn't count on you being a part of our group for the next assignment, in any case. Dana totally hates your guts,' he stated matter-of-factly.

Arjun laughed. 'Yeah, I figured that when she threatened to take my name off the assignment unless I paid for the printing of the assignment! I was like, "Damn, girl. Why so uptight?" She needs to get some action, am I right?'

When Zaid didn't reply, he continued. 'It's okay, though. I know a few other kids who'll take me in their group the next time. So anyway, you live in Glengarry right?'

'Yeah, I do.' He wanted this conversation to be done with so he could get to his room and sleep, but Arjun powered through.

'Cool, bro. I live in Dundee, five minutes from here. What are you up to this weekend by the way?'

'No major plans, as such. I was planning on sleeping for the most part.'

'Me too, bro. Me too. But a bunch of us are going downtown tomorrow night. We'll hit up a couple of clubs and bars. Why don't you come along? We'll pre-drink in my room and then head out. You in?'

'Ah, thanks, Arjun. I think I'm going to pass, but you guys have fun,' Zaid replied.

'You sure, bro? There'll be lots of pretty chicks at Van Gogh's tomorrow night. I swear, every Saturday, the hottest girls descend downtown. Like why do I never see them on campus, right? Listen, if you change your mind, just come to apartment 702 in Dundee tomorrow. Around nine,' Arjun said.

There was no way Zaid wanted to go out with Arjun and his pot-head friends, but he told Arjun he would think about it. He was about to turn and walk to his res. when he saw a pretty girl make her way up to them.

'Hey, you. What's happening?' she gushed as she hugged Arjun.

'Not much, beautiful! Fiona, this is Zaid. Zaid, meet Princess Fiona,' Arjun said.

Fiona giggled. 'Hey, Zaid. How's it going?'

Zaid greeted her back and waved as he turned to make his way to his apartment.

Fiona hardly noticed that he had left and continued giggling as Arjun regaled her with some story. Zaid could hear her squealing with laughter as he walked away.

'She has such a huge crush on him. And I'm pretty sure that he is leading her on. Ah, there's an innocent sucker for every douche,' Zaid thought as he entered the elevator.

He opened one eye and squinted at the time on the clock. It was twelve noon. Nice. It felt so good to be able to just sleep in and do nothing. He proceeded to spend the rest of the afternoon catching up on his favourite TV show,

Scandal. He had started watching the show because of Devi and then got hooked on it. She had also introduced him to the song '*Sweater Weather*' by the band, The Neighbourhood. He still played the song on loop every other day. Strange how someone can leave your life but ensure that they leave an indelible mark before they go. Devi was gone but her favourite songs and soaps were a part of his life for the foreseeable future.

He flipped through the apps on his phone and saw Instagram tucked away in one of the folders. He opened the app. Devi had introduced him to Instagram, too. In fact, she had written his bio. 'Star Wars nerd. Relatively awesome – if you don't believe me, ask my girlfriend.' He really ought to change that bio. He hadn't checked Instagram since he had come to Canada. Instinctively, he went through his newsfeed. He scrolled through random pictures of his friends and family. And then it happened. He saw her post. She had put it up just a few hours ago. The picture was captioned: 'Best night ever #thegoodlife #friends #love #happiness.' He stared at the picture for a long time. The asshole, Lyle, had his arms around her. Her best friends, Sue and Shana, flanked the happy couple. They were all laughing and looked like they had genuinely been having the time of their lives. He felt sick.

She was happy. She wasn't miserable like he had expected her to be. She didn't regret breaking his heart. She didn't care. She had trampled on his heart and then blithely moved on. While he, on the other hand, had cocooned himself from the world. He looked around at the empty crisps packets, pizza boxes and beer bottles littering his room. For the first time since he had moved to Canada, he realized just how lonely he was. He had no friends and he had no one to blame for that but himself. He needed to get a life and he needed to get one right away. He had wasted way too much time on an insensitive, selfish woman. He looked at his watch. It was 7.30 p.m. He remembered the stoner, Arjun's invite. Room 702, Dundee. For some reason, even though he had only been half-listening to Arjun, he remembered his apartment's name and number.

An hour later, Zaid stared at his reflection in the mirror. He had shaved after nearly three weeks. He was wearing a self-printed, navy-blue shirt with jeans and the new tan loafers that his mum had gifted him before he left Durban. This was the first time he was pulling them out of the closet since he arrived in Canada. He was by no means vain but he knew he looked good today. He grabbed a case of beer and headed out of his apartment. It was time to break out of this self-imposed exile.

'Argh! This is so hard. All of these cards are so funny:

'"Why do I hurt all over?"

'"Leprosy,"

'"Harry Potter erotica,"

'"Teaching a robot to love,"

'"Fiery poops,"

'"A bigger, blacker dick,"

'"Sneezing, farting and cumming at the same time,"

'"Dark and mysterious forces beyond our control," and

'"The Chinese gymnastics team,"' Fiona read from

the cards laid out on the carpet as everyone roared with laughter.

'Come on, Fi. Decide already,' Nat urged.

'Okay, okay. I'm going to go with "sneezing, farting and cumming at the same time",' she conceded.

'Yesss! Hand the card over, please. I'm so good at this game! And it's my first time playing it,' Zaid bellowed as everyone else yelled at Fiona for not choosing their cards.

Zaid added the card to his burgeoning pile of black cards. He was surprised at how much fun the night had turned out to be.

When he had rocked up at Arjun's apartment, he had been a little apprehensive. What if Arjun and his friends thought he was a complete loser for actually taking up his random invitation? But then he had brushed the thought aside. If he didn't feel welcome by Arjun and his friends, he could just leave and head downtown by himself. But when Arjun opened the apartment door, he greeted Zaid enthusiastically. 'Bro! You made it! And you brought beer. Sweet,' he said.

There were six people sprawled out across the couches in the apartment.

The pretty girl Zaid had met the previous day was chatting with another gorgeous girl. The rest of the group comprised of three guys and a girl.

'Guys, this is Zaid. Zaid, this is everyone. We're drinking here for another two hours and then heading downtown. And you're not just drinking beer. We're doing shots, Zaid,' Arjun announced.

By the time they headed downtown, Zaid was pretty

drunk. Arjun's friends were extremely friendly. Or maybe they were just really plastered too. The result was that Zaid felt like he had known them for ages. He laughed, danced and drank with the group at the three clubs they visited. Fiona even played wingman by introducing Zaid to girls at the clubs. Of all the people he was introduced to, Zaid felt attracted to only one. They danced at Van Gogh's and despite the loud music, he gathered that she was a second-year student on campus. They exchanged numbers before she had to leave and Zaid promised to call her. He smiled at her as she walked towards the exit. Zaid looked around to find Fiona. He wanted to thank her for all her efforts. He spotted her in a corner of the club. He carefully picked his way past the gyrating multitude and was just about to tap her on the shoulder, when Arjun suddenly drew her to himself and began kissing her.

'Uh, right. I guess I'll thank her later, then,' Zaid thought as he made his way back to the rest of the group at the bar.

When the clubs shut at 3.00 a.m., the party continued at Arjun's apartment. Someone brought the Cards Against Humanity game out and the laughter hadn't stopped since then.

The next morning Zaid woke up with the worst hangover he had ever had. An exploration of his wallet revealed that he had used up forty Canadian dollars the previous night. But an exploration of his phone revealed that he had been added to a WhatsApp group called 'Bros'.

'What an awesome night, guys. We have to do it again this week. Awesome meeting you, Zaid,' someone had written in the group.

At last, Zaid felt like a normal college kid. And a terrible headache and losing some money felt like a small price to pay for feeling normal again.

'So, I'm just like really done with like fake people and their unnecessary drama, you know what I mean?' Jane asked, looking at him expectantly.

Zaid had been lost in thought for a while now. He had no idea what she was talking about. He had to say something though, so he said, 'Uh ... yes, I agree.' It was a gamble saying that. After all, she could have said 'my friend just called me a bitch' for all he knew. Whatever it was, it seemed like replying in the affirmative was a good idea because Jane looked satisfied by his response. She continued to ramble on while Zaid struggled to focus on her words.

Before he could realize what was happening, his mind had taken him back to his first date with Devi. He had been extremely nervous. After all, he had had a crush on her for six months before he had actually done something about it and had asked her out. He could barely believe his luck when she had actually agreed to go out with him. He had been the one rambling on that date. He was so nervous that he had been absent-mindedly twiddling a drinking straw and had accidentally flicked it into her soup. Devi had looked startled for about five seconds before bursting into laughter. He had started laughing too and the date had gone smoothly from there. It was the most memorable evening of his life. In comparison to that evening, this date was a complete disaster. After taking her number on Saturday night, he had waited for two days before calling Jane. They had agreed to meet for coffee at Starbucks downtown. He glanced at his phone briefly. 7.45 p.m. This date had been on for just forty-five minutes and it already felt like a lifetime. He needed to escape. He excused himself to go to the loo where he spent a lot longer than he needed to just to kill some time. When he returned to the table, he resolved to end the date in the next ten minutes, no matter what.

'Jane, I'm having a great time with you, but I really have to head back. I only just remembered I've got an assignment due tomorrow!' He had always been a terrible liar and his sweaty palms and rapid speech were a dead giveaway.

She looked a bit suspicious, but smiled. 'Okay, sure. Let's head back to campus then. The bus will be here any minute now.'

'It's a group assignment. I have to meet Arjun here first and then we'll work on the assignment. Let me walk you to the door,' he urged.

If she didn't undersand what he was trying to do earlier, she definitely did now.

'No, that isn't required. I can get to the door by myself. Bye.' She stormed off.

He felt bad, but there was no point pretending that the date had gone off well. It was better this way. He knew one bad date wasn't the end of the world but he felt like crap. It was highly optimistic on his part to think that his first date after Devi would be perfect. But what if he never found the magic he had with Devi again? And was Jane really that boring? Or had he become so jaded that he could never like anyone again? Was he incapable of falling in love again?

He walked to the bus stop twenty minutes later. He barely waited for a minute before the next bus going to the university arrived. Although the bus was fairly full for a weeknight, he managed to find one seat. He stared out of the window as the bus zipped through the streets. It jerked to a halt at the next stop, propelling him forward and snapping him out of his reverie. He cursed under his breath. Only one girl boarded the bus. It was the girl from the mixer. Rachel? Rachna? She walked towards him, her eyes scanning the bus for a vacant seat. She didn't find any and sighed. She was tiny (about 5'2"); she had a pleasant face, her nose was rather large (it kind of dominated her face) but she had really beautiful upturned eyes. It was strange; he'd seen her before but he'd never really noticed her before. As if sensing his eyes on her, her eyes met his. Her face hardened. He had been an ass to her twice already; however, since he had resolved to be his normal, friendly self, he smiled at her. She looked confused. He smiled even wider. He stood up and gestured for her to take his seat.

'Thanks, but I'm fine. Uni isn't too far now. I can stand,' she said.

'Please take the seat. I'm tired of sitting anyway,' he replied.

She eyed him with suspicion and sat down. She probably wondered why he was being nice to her. She must have pegged him as an uptight jerk. He stood near her wondering what he should say next. He had been so rude to her the last two times that he had met her, that he didn't know how to ease the tension. He decided it would be best if he simply apologized for his past behaviour. He was just about to break the uncomfortable silence, when her phone rang. She picked it up and spoke cheerily.

'Hello? Oh, my God, Jo! I'm so happy to hear your voice! I miss you guys, man! What are you doing? Aw! That sounds like so much fun…'

She continued talking for the next ten minutes. When they reached campus, she rose and briskly got off the bus.

He watched her walk away and felt remorse. He didn't know what it was, but his gut told him that he needed to make things okay with her.

OCTOBER

'Later, Z! I'm seeing you at Kirsten's tomorrow, yeah?' Mark asked Zaid.

Zaid nodded, fist-bumped him and left class. He headed straight to Arjun's apartment. Hanging out with Arjun and his friends had become the norm ever since he had gone out with them for the first time two weeks ago. He regretted isolating himself for the first few days of campus and missing out on so much, but he was glad he was making the most of it now. He had started talking to people in all of his classes too. He realized that Canadians were really friendly, in general. You could start a conversation with anyone anywhere and the person wouldn't think you were crazy or flirting with him or her!

Things were different back home at his university in Durban. People generally belonged to cliques that were pretty hard to break into.

He was almost at Arjun's when he noticed tiny white blobs falling from the sky. It couldn't be! It wasn't supposed to snow for another month! People all around him held their palms out to feel the flakes. So, it was what he thought it was! It was snowing! The red and orange hued leaves on the trees around him were slowly getting coated with a film of white. The seasons were merging and it was incredibly beautiful. He clicked a picture and sent it to his mum. She had noticed that he was beginning to sound more like his old self in the last two weeks and had mentioned it to him.

He reached Arjun's apartment and was about to knock on the door when it opened. Fiona was on her way out. She was wearing the same jersey and jeans Zaid had seen her in the previous day. Her hair was messy and she wore a caught-in-the-act expression.

'Oh, hey, Z! What are you doing here so early in the morning?' she asked.

'Arjun and I have a test tomorrow so we're studying together,' Zaid replied.

'Cool, cool. Good luck. I'll leave you guys to it. I was just here to … uh … return Arjun's jacket. He lent it to me yesterday. Okay, bye,' Fiona explained.

'Sure, of course. See ya, Fi,' Zaid replied.

He spent the rest of the day trying to study with Arjun. Arjun was, of course, the worst person in the world he could have chosen to study with. He kept taking food and joint breaks, checking his phone and rating all the girls he knew.

'Fiona is an eight, Natalie is a nine and a half, but Rose – Rose is a definite ten. She's that rare mix of a stunning face and a banging body,' Arjun concluded.

'Right. And I guess you're planning to bang Rose soon then?'

'Planning to? Been there, done that, my friend.' Arjun smiled placidly.

'But Fiona is your latest conquest, right? Listen, I usually mind my own business, but Fi is a really sweet girl. She really likes you; it's written all over her face. So, if you're not serious about her, I don't think you should lead her on. I know what it's like to have your heart broken. I would hate to see that happen to her,' Zaid said.

'Zaid, Zaid, Zaid, you sound just like my older brother. Don't worry about Fiona. She is a grown up. I never promised her anything. She knows what she is getting into. And if she wants to get into bed with me, why should I say no? That will probably hurt her more! We're all adults here. And of course, I'm not serious about Fi! I'm not serious about anything right now. It's my first year at uni, bro. I'm here to have a good time. That's it.'

Zaid realized that he wasn't going to get through to Arjun. He had tried and that was all that he could really do. Perhaps he could have a chat with Fiona though and prepare her for what was bound to happen?

'Okay, bro, enough talk. Let's go eat. I'm starving,' Arjun announced. They headed to the food court on campus. As soon as they reached the food court, people started greeting Arjun.

'Bro, you're going to get a sub, yeah? Get me a Chicken Teriyaki, please. Here's my card,' Arjun said as he headed over to a table full of people he knew.

Zaid knew the benefits of socializing, but still wondered how Arjun managed to socialize so much. Didn't he ever feel the need to switch off?

Five minutes later, Zaid carried the food-laden tray to the table where he had last seen Arjun, but he wasn't there. He was off chatting up some pretty girl, Zaid assumed.

He scanned the room and as suspected, saw Arjun talking to a girl. Her back was to Zaid so he couldn't see her face, but he knew Arjun's preferences well enough to deduce that she must be pretty hot. As he neared them, Arjun spotted him and waved him over.

'This is my friend, Zaid. Zaid, meet Rachna,' Arjun said when Zaid reached the table.

Rachna turned around and Zaid was surprised to see the same girl from Australia with whom he had had various encounters.

'I know Zaid. Hi,' Rachna replied coldly.

'Hey, how are you doing?' Zaid asked.

'Great. Actually, I was just leaving.' She turned to Arjun and smiled warmly. 'Really nice meeting you, Arjun. I'll see you around.'

'Oh, you definitely will. What's your number, by the way?'

Wow! Arjun wasted no time. Zaid watched silently as Rachna and Arjun exchanged numbers. He was used to girls completely ignoring him in Arjun's presence, but Rachna's indifference bothered him. She glanced over her shoulder and gazed gooey-eyed at Arjun before making her way out. Zaid recognized that look; he had seen Fiona look at Arjun like that. He knew it was none of his business, but he couldn't let Rachna fall for Arjun's charms. He had to do something about this.

The next day, he stood at the entrance of the food court and surveyed the groups of students laughing and eating. It took him a few seconds before he spotted her. She was with a friend today. It was the same girl who had accompanied her to the screening of the *Blind Side* a few weeks ago. He rubbed his sweaty palms together. He hadn't counted on her being with someone. After all, only yesterday, she had been here alone. Just his luck! It wasn't going to be easy to approach her with her friend around. The very same friend at whom he had snapped at during the movie screening. Fuck.

Nevertheless, he knew he had to talk to her, and soon. Arjun moved quickly and if he didn't talk to her now, the next time Zaid saw her, she would probably be sneaking out of Arjun's apartment. He took a deep breath and made his way to Rachna's table.

She was giggling at something her friend said. But, when she caught sight of Zaid, a scowl replaced her smile.

'Um … hi … Rachna. Hi,' he greeted both the girls at the table.

'Hi,' Rachna replied. It appeared that that monosyllable was all he was going to get from her. She stared at him enquiringly. He knew what she was thinking. 'What the hell does he want from me now?'

He cleared his throat. 'Uh, I wanted to talk to you about something important. But I need to speak with you in private.'

Rachna's friend said, 'Fine. I need to get water in any case,' and left the table.

He wondered how to broach the topic. She stared at

him pointedly and he knew she was getting impatient. He decided to come straight to the point.

'So, this is about Arjun.' He paused and noticed her eyebrows go up. She was definitely interested in what he had to say now. 'He is my friend and is really fun to hang out with. But there is something you should know. He is a charmer. He flirts with many women simultaneously. So, you might think that he likes you, but just know that you're just an option for him. I'm only telling you all of this because I don't want to see you get hurt,' he concluded.

She gaped at him for a moment before speaking. 'Zaid, are you on drugs?'

What? Of all of the possible things she could say, that was so not the response he had expected.

'Excuse me? What do you mean?' he replied.

'What I mean is, there is definitely something wrong with you! The first time I met you, I was super-friendly and chatty and you gave me the cold shoulder. It was my first day in Canada; all I was looking for was a friend and you were so, so rude to me. The very next time I saw you, you yelled at my friend and me for enjoying ourselves during a movie. So, I'm sure you understand why I thought you were an uptight ass. Then suddenly you act all nice and offer your seat on the bus to me. And now you've come to warn me about a guy because you "care" about my feelings? Or is it because you think I'm not hot enough for your friend? He couldn't possibly really like me. I'm just an "option" for him, right? And this guy is your friend! Why would you go about badmouthing your own friend? I really don't know what your deal is, but I'm a grown up. I can take care of myself. I don't need you to tell me who I should or shouldn't be friendly with. You're probably jealous of Arjun's charisma and personality, but talking shit about your friend behind his back is pretty low,' she said.

Wow. She had got both him and his intentions completely wrong. He considered defending himself, but realized that it would be pointless. She had already made up her mind about him. She hated his guts, that was for sure.

Rachna's friend was back with her bottle of water and Zaid took it as his cue to leave.

He could hear Rachna filling her friend in on the conversation he had just had with her as he walked away.

'He said WHAT? Oh, my God! What a weirdo!' he heard her friend say.

He quickened his pace so he could get the hell out of the food court. Maybe he had it right when he first moved to Canada and didn't care about anyone. People were just not worth it.

It was Saturday night again. Arjun and gang had headed downtown to party. Zaid had gotten used to partying every weekend. He always had a good time when he went out with the gang. After the dismal date with the girl he met in the club three weeks ago, he chose not to look for anything serious when he went out. He drank, danced and kissed girls (okay, it had just been two girls so far. He wasn't turning into Arjun, not anytime soon anyway...)

in the club, but never expected anything else. He was enjoying being young and single.

'Here you go. One vodka and coke,' the pretty bartender at Van Gogh's handed Zaid his drink. He paid her the exact amount and turned around. He was about to walk towards the couches where Arjun, Fiona and gang were seated when he saw Rachna at the far end of the room. She had just entered the club with her friends. She was dressed in a short black dress. Her hair looked sleek. She had clearly dressed to impress. She looked amazing. Zaid couldn't take his eyes off her.

The song '*Lean on*' started up. Rachna and her friends got super excited and began dancing where they were by the door. Rachna swayed her hips to match the beat of the song. Hot damn! She was a really good dancer. The song ended and the DJ played an unfamiliar song. Rachna and friends didn't recognize it either; they stopped swaying and made their way to the bar. Zaid contemplated going outside so that he could avoid her; if she saw him, she would probably accuse him of stalking her. And that was when it happened. Rachna noticed Arjun. Arjun was kissing Fiona passionately. His hands were on her hips. His eyes were shut so he was oblivious to Rachna's presence. Rachna whispered something in her friend's ear and quickly walked out into the outdoor terrace area of the club.

Zaid followed her. She was by the balustrade, looking at the skyline. He hesitated for a few seconds, but then went up to her.

'Hey. Are you okay?' he asked as he stood directly behind her.

She turned around and frowned. 'Oh, you again. Yes, I'm fine. Why?'

'Uh … I'm guessing you saw Arjun and Fiona now…'

'Yes, I did. And I see that you were right about Arjun, so you can gloat if you like. But I just want to be on my own now.' She looked at him pointedly.

'Yes, of course. Take care.' He turned to walk away, but something stopped him and he said, 'I'll totally understand if you say "no" given how our past encounters have gone down, but I really would like to meet you for coffee sometime. We got off on the wrong foot and if you give me a chance, I might just surprise you,' he said.

She looked a little taken aback. 'Well, I'm done with guys surprising me.' She gestured to the spot indoors where Arjun was. 'I would rather a guy just be upfront about things. But sure, what the hell, we can do coffee. Does Monday evening work for you?'

Zaid had an important test on Tuesday but he didn't want to reschedule in case Rachna changed her mind about going out with him altogether.

'Yeah, sure. That works. I'll see you then.'

She inspected herself in the mirror. She was wearing a bright orange, open shoulder top, skinny jeans and brogues. She added her fitted grey jacket on top. It was only October but the temperature had already started dipping. 'Okay. So, I guess I'm ready for whatever-this-is with Zaid,' she thought.

She had been open to meeting guys on campus but her love life remained pretty uneventful. She had been on coffee dates with two guys so far. The first guy had seemed promising. The conversation was great, he was funny and they shared a common love of reading. She expected to hear from him right after their date. But when he let a whole week go by before calling her, she reckoned he wasn't that interested in her after all. She nevertheless gave him a second chance and went out with him again. However, when he pulled the same stunt again, she realized their 'relationship' was going nowhere. The next time he called her, she ignored it. He didn't try to get in touch again and that was the end of that.

The next guy she met was just extremely dull. She kept wishing she was in her room reading or watching a show on Netflix while she was on the date with him, and that was obviously not a good sign.

When she met Arjun a few days ago, she was instantly attracted to him. She was pretty hopeful when she exchanged numbers with him. However, when he had had her number for three days and hadn't called, she was bummed. Nevertheless when she went out on Saturday, she had told herself that she would wait until Monday to see if he called her. And then she saw him making out with some girl.

So, when she headed out to meet Zaid, she had no expectations at all. She was surprised he had even asked her out, but then again he had proven to be pretty moody and strange ever since she had met him. In any case, she had already plumbed the depths of awful dates with boring guys, so she figured it couldn't get any worse than that.

When she reached Tim Hortons, he was already seated at a table. He smiled and waved when he saw her. She gave him a small smile and walked over to the table. He immediately stood up and pulled out a chair for her.

'Thank you. Sorry, I'm a little late,' she said.

'Not at all. So, what would you like? The cheesecake here is amazing by the way,' he said.

'Ooh. Yeah, I think I'll try the blueberry cheesecake then. And a café latte. Thanks.'

'Sure. I'll just go and place our order,' he said immediately.

Five minutes later, he returned with a tray with two steaming hot café lattes, a blueberry cheesecake and a baked Philadelphia cheesecake.

'Yum!' She took a bite of the cheesecake and instantly felt her mood lighten.

'So ...' he said.

'So ...' she said.

'I don't want to sound cheesy and I know this isn't a movie but I really hope we can start over. This is what I should have said when we met for the first time last month: "Hi, I'm Zaid. I'm from Durban, South Africa. I'm usually a fun-loving guy and an extremely loyal friend. But I ... uh ... I recently experienced heartbreak and that has unfortunately made me really bitter. I'm actually dead on the inside",' he said, sombrely.

She raised an eyebrow and Zaid laughed.

'Well, I'm fine now – maybe not a hundred per cent

okay, but I'm getting there. But when you met me last month, I was grouchy for a reason.'

She was intrigued now. 'Wow, okay. So why did it end with your ex? Actually, sorry, that was too personal – you don't have to answer that,' she said.

'No, it's okay. I can finally talk about it now. My ex cheated on me. We dated for two years. She was the love of my life. Or at least, I thought she was. And I walked in on her with another guy.'

'Woah! Your life really is like a movie. So, you actually walked in on them ... you know ... doing it?'

'God, no! That would have been super traumatic. But it was close. When she opened the door to her flat, she looked really guilty. And when I walked into the bathroom, he was standing in her bathtub with a towel wrapped around his waist. A towel that I had gifted her, by the way.'

'Ouch. I'm not justifying her behaviour but maybe she thought your relationship wouldn't last once you came to Canada to study. Perhaps she thought it was inevitable that the relationship would end, and that was why she cheated on you.'

He shook his said to say no. 'It was only after I caught her cheating on me that I decided to come to Canada. I had no intention of leaving Durban before that. When I figured I was still completely messed up even three months after the break up, I realized I needed to get out of Durban. We were at the same uni. And even if we hadn't gone to the same college, I would have still seen her around the city. There isn't that much to do in Durban.

I was bound to see her at the beach or at the mall or something. And I couldn't stand to see her.'

'Oh. What made you choose Canada though?'

'I found out about the exchange programmes on campus. Canada was just one of the options. I had also considered Australia. In the end, Canada was what worked out.'

She nodded. 'I kinda left Australia because I wanted to get away too. Not from a guy but just from the life I knew there. It was pretty much the same grind every day and it suddenly dawned on me that I was young and I deserved to lead an exciting life!'

He grinned. 'Yes, you do. We all do.'

'So ... um ... why did you decide to start being nice to me? I mean, what triggered the realization that you had been, for want of a better word, an ass to me?'

He laughed. 'Well for the first few weeks since campus started, I had been keeping to myself. Just focusing on my classes and assignments. I didn't bother making any friends, nothing. I was like a crazy person living in a bubble. And then one day I saw a picture of Devi on Instagram, the ex, you know, with that douche, Lyle, the bathtub guy. And they looked really happy. In fact, her hashtags revealed that she had had the "best night ever". That was my wake-up call. I realized I had stopped living my life and she didn't even care. I mean, after we broke up and before I moved to Canada, I had seen her a few times on campus and she hadn't exactly looked devastated then, but I had purposely tried to stay away from any news of her at that time. But she had messaged me and tried calling me, so I assumed she felt some remorse.'

Rachna nodded. 'And when you saw her picture, you realized that she had moved on with that ass and you had been left behind.'

'Exactly! And as it were, I had just met Arjun the day before and he had invited me to hang with his friends and him. So, I decided to start acting like a normal person. I went out with Arjun, Fiona and the rest of them and had a great time. I started becoming my old self. And so, when I saw you in the bus again, I tried making up for the times I had been a jerk,' Zaid concluded.

Rachna smiled at him. When she had come out today, she had expected nothing from this meeting, but it was proving to be the best date she had had so far. That comfortable vibe that she had thought was completely missing the first time she met Zaid was now fully present. They sat at the coffee shop for two hours and spoke about everything under the sun – books, movies, TV, their goals and dreams, and more.

She didn't know if it would lead to anything, but she knew she had found what she was looking for when she had first greeted him a month ago – a friend.

Zaid walked into the library resolutely. He had tonnes of studying to do. Studying with Arjun had proved to be singularly pointless. Plus, with his new found social life, he had fallen behind with his studies. He had three very important tests coming up and he needed to ace them. He decided to go up to the studying area on the second floor.

He would find a quiet cubicle and study, study, study. No interruptions. No distractions. He waited for the elevator. The doors opened and she emerged.

'Oh, hey! What's up?' she greeted him.

'Hey yourself. Are you stalking me again, Rachna? I know I'm hard to resist, but come on,' Zaid teased.

'You got me! You're right; you're irresistible, Zaid. It's that sexy South African accent of yours,' she quipped.

He knew she was joking, but his heart skipped a beat.

'So, what's happening?' he asked.

'Don't ask! I'm dying! I have a forty-page assignment due tomorrow. I'm going to have to pull an all-nighter. I was just going to the café to grab a bite. I'm starving. Are you hungry?'

He had just eaten a sub on his way to the library but he didn't want to pass up an opportunity to hang out with her.

'I can eat. Let's go,' he replied.

Forty-five minutes later, they were back at the library. He accompanied her to the second floor. He took a seat next to her and opened his text book.

'How many pages have you done?' he asked her.

'Seventeen. So, I'm half-way there, right? Sort of?' she asked hopefully.

'Yeah, for sure. Almost done. Hang in there,' he replied.

'Ha ha, as if. But thanks for the encouragement,' she smiled.

He had barely read one line from his text book when she gasped.

'Oh shit. No, no, no! You stupid, stupid laptop,' she cried.

'What happened?' he asked, concerned.

'I didn't save the last five pages I wrote! And it didn't get auto-saved either. I don't know what happened. I thought I had saved it. My brain is turning to mush. I think I accidentally saved the older version of the document and the latest stuff I had typed got replaced.'

Her heart started pounding. It was already 9.00 p.m. She wasn't going to be able to finish this assignment in time. She was already exhausted. Her arms hurt from all the typing she had been doing. Before she knew it, her eyes welled up.

'Rachna, hey, come on, don't cry.' Zaid put his arm around her. 'Shit happens. You can't waste time crying about what is lost. You have to move ahead.'

'I don't want to move ahead! I can't do this shit! I'm so tired. My arms hurt!' she replied, frustrated.

'Rach, take a deep breath. I'll type for you, okay? You just tell me what you want to write.'

She smiled a small smile. 'That's really sweet, Zaid. But you have your own shit to do. You just told me how much studying *you* have to do. I can't waste your time.'

He looked into her eyes and said, 'Trust me; you're not wasting my time. At all. I want to do this. Let me help you.'

By 1.00 a.m., they had managed to finish a total of twenty-five pages.

'Wow! You type fast!' Rachna said as Zaid completed the twenty-fifth page.

'Well, we're working on panic mode, aren't we? No time to rest!' Zaid replied.

Rachna looked at her watch. 'Ah, but the library will close in five minutes. Thank you so much, Zaid. I really don't know what I would have done if you weren't here. You're an absolute life saver!'

'Anytime, Rach. But the assignment isn't complete yet. Let's continue at your apartment.' Zaid suggested.

She stared at him for a few seconds unable to respond, post which she quickly said, 'No, no, don't worry, Zaid. I've got it from here. I'll be fine.'

'Don't worry. We'll only do work at your apartment. I know you'll find it hard to resist me but I can take care of myself. I won't let you molest me,' Zaid mocked.

Rachna rolled her eyes. 'In your dreams, Z! Okay, if you're sure. Let's go.'

They braved the cold wind and walked to Rachna's apartment in comfortable silence. 'I'm going to make tea,' Rachna volunteered when they reached the apartment. Zaid accompanied her to the kitchen. She extracted a pot from the cupboard above the sink. Zaid noticed that it had crumbs along the rim.

'I … uh … I'll just wash it again.' Rachna rinsed the pot and Zaid smiled. She had missed quite a few spots.

An hour later, Zaid was busy typing when Rachna emerged with two bowls of noodles from the kitchen.

'Did you make the noodles in the same pot that you made the tea in?' Zaid asked.

'Yeah, but I washed the pot! Why?'

'Because the noodles taste of tea,' Zaid chuckled.

'How is that possible? You're just being anal,' Rachna tried defending herself. But she looked into Zaid's eyes and they both began laughing uncontrollably.

'Rachna Rai, I'm going to have to say it. You're a complete slob!'

'All I can say is, I'm glad you haven't seen my room yet,' Rachna smiled.

'I have to see it now! Show it to me!' he urged.

'No way in hell!' she replied.

'You told me you owe me for helping you today. Well, this is what I want in return for helping you! I want to see your room.'

'That's low! Argh! I guess I have no option but to show it to you now. Fine, I'll show it to you. But you can't judge me. As you know, things have been hectic!'

She opened her room door and Zaid's mouth fell open. There were clothes strewn all over her bed and her cupboard was open and overflowing. Her desk was covered with biscuit packet wrappers, crisps, pouches and make-up in addition to the books.

'Wow! I'm speechless. This is by far, the messiest room I have ever seen.'

'Whatever! It's not that bad. And come on, let's get back to work! You said it yourself; we're on panic mode.'

Zaid chuckled. 'Sure, change the topic but the damage is already done. I think I'm going to have nightmares about your room,' Zaid teased.

'Well, it's a good thing you're not getting any sleep tonight then,' Rachna quipped.

They spent the next five hours completing Rachna's assignment. They shared stories from their childhood with each other as they worked.

Zaid told Rachna about Sunday lunches at his aunt's house; a weekly ritual in which he had participated ever since he was born. He told her how much he missed seeing his cousins (and there were a lot of them) every week. Rachna told Zaid about Jo, Amy, Aisha, her dad and about her mum's 'zen' attitude to life.

At 6.00 a.m., Zaid added the final full stop to the assignment and smiled with satisfaction.

'And it's done. We did it! Go team,' he said as he raised his hand for a high five.

Rachna looked into his eyes and pulled him into a tight embrace instead. He felt his heart thump as he wrapped his arms around her. He couldn't help notice how well she fitted into his shoulder nook. He inhaled her scent; she smelled like jasmine and citrus all at once. He didn't want to let her go.

'I can't believe you stayed up all night with me to complete my assignment, Zaid. This is the nicest thing anyone has ever done for me. Like ever. Please let me know how I can return the favour. Seriously,' she said, still hugging him.

'Oh, come on, Rach. It's no big deal. We both know how lonely living away from home can be. It's important to have at least one person you know you can count on. I'm glad I could be that person for you,' he smiled.

'I'm glad you could be that person for me too,' she replied.

She pulled away just enough to look at him. They still had their arms around each other. The first rays of the morning fell upon them through the window. The birds began chirping. He felt as if time stood still. They looked into each other's eyes. He leaned in towards her. He was going to kiss her. She was about to close her eyes when her roommate, Serena walked into the room.

'Hey, Rach. You're up early,' Serena said, eyeing Zaid.

'Oh, uh, yeah. Major assignment due today. This is Zaid, by the way. Zaid, meet Serena.'

Zaid greeted her and then said, 'Okay, I'm off. I'll go sleep a bit. Luckily, my first class is at eleven.'

Rachna bit her lip. Damn Serena and her terrible timing! Oh well, another time. And when Zaid turned to glance at her before walking out of the door, she was sure there would be another time.

'Okay so everyone, have your pages ready by tomorrow. Ryan, you're doing the SWOT analysis and Business Plan, right? We'll meet at the same time in the library and put it together,' Dana said.

'I am? What does SWOT stand for again? Substantial Waste of Time?' Ryan replied.

Dana's eyes widened. She looked genuinely shocked although everyone else giggled.

'Dana, don't have a heart attack. I was kidding. Yup, I'm on it. See you guys tomorrow,' Ryan said as he rose from the table.

‘That wasn’t funny,’ Dana muttered, gathering her belongings from the desk.

Tia rolled her eyes and locked eyes with Zaid. He grinned.

They walked out of the library together.

‘Dana is just so ... she’s just ...’ Tia struggled to complete her sentence.

‘She is just Dana. There is definitely no one like her,’ Zaid nodded. ‘What else is going on? Are you coming to the Indian Students’ Association mixer thingie next Saturday?’

‘Yeah, for sure. Is your crew going to be there?’ Tia asked.

‘Yup. Arjun, Fiona, Rachna; everyone’s really excited about it. You know Arjun already, but you’ll get to meet everyone else on Saturday,’ Zaid said.

Tia rolled her eyes at the mention of Arjun’s name. Zaid noticed and laughed.

‘You know you’re one of the few girls on campus who doesn’t have a crush on Arjun. You and Dana, maybe,’ Zaid said.

‘Yeah, ’cos he’s an idiot. I can’t believe girls can’t see through his bullshit. Okay, I’m off. See you tomorrow. And listen I’ll hardly know anyone at the mixer so you better hang with me on Saturday, Mr Sociable,’ Tia replied.

Zaid nodded and waved at Tia as she walked away.

In what world was he Mr Sociable? But he had had a pretty eventful month. He had been going to pub quiz nights downtown, he had joined the Indian Students’

Association and had been attending their events, and he had also been going to a lot of parties. He was amazed at the number of cool people there were on campus. Tia had been part of his assignment group in New Product Development although he hadn't interacted with her much before. However, in the last week, they had been working for long hours on a group assignment and he had gotten to know her fairly well.

She wanted to meet more people because she was homesick for Mumbai. He suggested she join the Indian Students' Association and she was more than happy to be a part of it.

He wondered what Rachna was up to. He was about to dial her number when he got a call on his phone.

'Hey? What's wrong? Why are you crying? Don't cry ... it will be okay ... yes I'll be at mine in five minutes ... come over,' he spoke into the phone.

He sighed and rushed off.

She had had an amazing time in Toronto over the weekend. When her friend, Leigh, had invited her to spend Thanksgiving with her family in Toronto, Tia had been hesitant. The campus grew rather desolate over the weekends as students from the nearby towns and cities returned to their homes. Tia hung out with the international students during such times and for the most part, it was fun. However, Thanksgiving weekend was going to be more deserted than usual. Everyone wanted to use the long weekend to travel out of Guelph. She hadn't travelled around Toronto and she figured this was her chance.

Leigh's parents were very warm and Tia watched as they engulfed her in bear hugs when they came to pick her up. You'd have thought that they were seeing their daughter after ages; when in reality it was just a week. The hour-long journey to Toronto was enlivened by Leigh's mother filling Leigh in on that week's events. Leigh had told Tia that her mother was her best friend and Tia could see that now. Tia felt a pang. Although she had been speaking to her mother on the phone regularly, the grudge she still held towards her parents stopped her from being warm with her mother. She hardly spoke with her father and when she did, she kept her responses short.

Plus, she had been so busy with her job, classes and socializing, that she had barely given any thought to how her parents were really doing without her. As she watched Leigh and her mum chatter away incessantly, she suddenly realized how lonely her parents must feel without her. The house must feel really empty. She remembered the time her mother travelled to Dubai for a month to spend time with *Masi*. The house had become so quiet; she hadn't even realized her dad was home sometimes. She made a mental note to call her mother and speak at length with her after the weekend.

On Friday evening, Leigh took Tia out for dinner with her friends. She met three of Leigh's closest school friends. Leigh and her friends reminisced about their school days. Their stories and conversation reminded Tia of Armaan, Neha and Stan. Even though she didn't know all their inside jokes, and all the jokes had to be explained to Tia, she was glad that she didn't feel excluded as tight-knit groups can sometimes make outsiders feel. Leigh's friends were welcoming and by the end of the night, Tia felt like she had known them forever. After dinner, one of Leigh's friends suggested that they go to the all-ages club downtown. Tia was nineteen and hence considered of legal age when it came to entering clubs in Canada, but Leigh and her friends were eighteen and therefore, a 'real' club was out of the question for them. The plan was that Tia would score drinks for all the girls since she had her ID with her. As soon as the five of them entered the club, they were approached (or rather hounded) by the guys in the club. Although the girls shooed the guys away saying that they weren't interested in twerking or grinding with them, Tia could tell that the girls were secretly enjoying all the attention. Tia couldn't help but feel cool compared to these naïve girls: she had been free to party to no end with her friends back home (albeit with the strict curfews imposed by her parents).

An ugly, old (he must have been forty, at least) guy started grinding with one of Leigh's friends, Sharon. Ugh! What kind of creep comes to an all-ages club when he is forty and hits on underage teenage girls? Sharon made eye contact with her friends who all gestured to her that the guy was not really worth it. But by then Sharon was so drunk, she couldn't see how ugly he actually was. She continued to dance with the guy as her friends looked helplessly on. Eventually, tired of fending off all the unwelcome advances, Tia climbed onto a table so she could dance in peace. Leigh and her friends, having had their fill of dancing with sleazebags, joined her up on the table too. The girls were enjoying themselves when an Indian guy in his thirties climbed onto their table as well. Probably in an alcohol-induced haze, he imagined that he was Akshay Kumar in a Bollywood song being fawned over by starstuck groupies. He miserably failed of course as none of the girls paid any heed to him. Eventually he got off the table as the girls cracked up. Overall, it was one of the most enjoyable nights Tia had had since she got to Canada.

The next morning, Tia was woken up by a flurry of activity at Leigh's place. It was Thanksgiving Day and Leigh's parents were busy preparing a huge meal for their family. Leigh was helping her mother peel potatoes in the kitchen while Leigh's father expertly prepared the turkey for stuffing. Tia, never keen on domestic activities, had no option but to volunteer her services too, although fortunately for her, Leigh and her folks didn't need her help. Having dutifully chopped twenty potatoes, Leigh decided to take Tia downtown to see the famous CN Tower, the ice rink and other sights. Tia was the quintessential tourist – taking selfies outside every possible building. Leigh proved to be a good sport – acting as excited as Tia, despite having seen everything in the city innumerable times.

They finally headed home an hour before the lavish Thanksgiving dinner was served. They were greeted by Leigh's aunts, uncles and cousins when they reached her place. Tia was soaking their traditions right in. When she sat at the long table laden with the specially prepared meal, she savoured the experience. Something she had only ever seen on *Friends*, the *Big Bang Theory* and *How I Met Your Mother*, was finally unfolding in front of her eyes. She enjoyed her first Thanksgiving although, truth be told, she found the taste of turkey, rather weird. She'd pick chicken over turkey any day, thank you very much.

On Sunday, Leigh took her to the annual street parade. With people dressed in various costumes dancing to lilting music, the carnival was a riot of colour and sound.

Tia had a very important test scheduled for the following Tuesday and although she had carried her books along with the virtuous intention of studying over the weekend, she hadn't really gotten down to it. This was the only blot on her otherwise perfect horizon. However, the ambience and mood was so festive that Tia couldn't help forgetting her worries and enjoying herself.

After the parade, Leigh and Tia had a late lunch at a café downtown and then went shopping at Eaton Centre. Tia hadn't shopped ever since she reached Canada. She needed a warm coat, for starters.

'Winter is coming, my friend! This flimsy jacket of yours is not going to protect you from the harsh winds and the freezing temperatures,' Leigh declared dramatically.

They spent hours trying to find something suitable because, as Leigh put it, 'it was a big commitment'. Tia would be stuck with the coat for a long time and she needed to ensure that she found 'the one'.

They finally did succeed in Mission Bomber Jacket. She found a black zip-up bomber duffle coat that was warm but also stylish. Leigh managed to convince her to buy another calf-length, red winter trench coat as well. Tia was delighted with her purchases; she had forgotten what an exhilarating high shopping brought with it. But when she looked at her watch, she shrieked. 'It's late! It's nine-thirty already! I've got to get to your place, pack and then leave for Guelph again. And the last bus leaves Toronto at eleven!'

They rushed back to Leigh's place and Tia made it to the bus stop at 10.50 p.m. managing to buy the bus ticket in the nick of time. She thanked Leigh's father and Leigh for the wonderful weekend and boarded the bus.

Her phone rang as soon as the bus set off. It was Zaid.

'Hey, you! How was Thanksgiving weekend?' he asked cheerfully.

'Fabulous! And yours? What's up?'

'Mine was pretty awesome too. We chilled at Natalie's place in Toronto. I just got back to campus a few hours ago,' he replied.

'Oh, cool. I'm actually on my way back to Guelph now. I think I'll reach the bus stop downtown by midnight.'

'Ooh, that's late. You know what? I'm actually doing dinner at Caribou Creek now. I'll probably finish by twelvish too. Do you want me to meet you at the bus stop? We could take a cab back to campus together?' he offered.

'Oh, that would be perfect. I'll see you at twelve then?'

'Yup! Just give me a call when you're ten minutes away and I'll start walking towards the stop,' he told her.

'Guelph. This stop is Guelph,' an automated voice in the bus announced.

She opened her eyes. She had fallen asleep in the bus. She looked at her watch. It was 12.15 a.m. The drive had taken longer than usual. And she hadn't called Zaid because she had fallen asleep. Shit! She dialled his number but his phone was switched off.

The doors of the bus swished open and seven people, including Tia, got out. There was a family of four and two young girls. Tia disembarked with her case and stood at the station. She kept trying Zaid's number, but his phone was clearly not coming back on any time soon. His battery must have died. A car drew up and picked up the family. She considered befriending the two girls standing at the stop, and wondered whether they were en route to the campus as well. 'Are you heading to the university?' she asked the girls.

'Oh, no. We're still in school. We're going home to Alberta Street.'

Crap. A car came to collect the girls and off they went.

Alone at the bus stop, Tia wondered what to do. She clicked on the Uber app on her phone, but it simply wouldn't open. Damn! This was not a good time for her phone to hang. Muttering under her breath, she restarted her phone and watched in despair as the app took forever to come alive. When it finally did, she booked a cab. She called the driver who informed her that it would take him about ten minutes to get there. The street was deserted. Downtown was busy on Saturday nights, but quiet on Sunday nights. And since it was Thanksgiving weekend and students were still out of town, it was like a ghost town that night. The light behind the display, which illuminated the bus stop, blinked a couple of times before blinking out altogether. Her heart skipped a beat. She was now plunged into total darkness at the bus stop.

She suddenly heard humming. She looked to her left to see three men who, in the faint light afforded by the night sky, looked like derelicts, walking towards her. They weaved and swayed, and were obviously drunk. She could feel her heart thump uncomfortably inside her chest. This was it. Something bad was going to happen to her. Away from home, in a foreign land. She couldn't help thinking that if her parents had been in Zaid's place, they'd have called her on their own to check where she was. A situation like this would never have arisen if her parents were around.

She began praying in her head. The hobos were getting closer when she heard a car. She looked in the direction of the sound and sure enough, her taxi was nosing its way into the bus terminus towards her. Thank you, God, thank you, God, thank you, God! The cab pulled up and she jumped in, relief flooding through her. The cab set off towards the university when her phone began to ring. It was Zaid.

'Hey. I'm so sorry. I lost track of time. I was wondering why you hadn't called. And then I looked at my phone and realized that it was dead. Just charged it. Where are you? Are you okay?' he asked.

She explained her whereabouts to him and he asked her if she could pick him up from where he was. It turned out that he was just a lane away. When he got into the cab, he said, 'I'm really sorry, Tia. That was bloody irresponsible on my part.'

'You know, just before this cab showed up, there were these three drunks walking towards me. It was really scary. Your phone was switched off and I didn't know what was going to happen. And the whole time, I couldn't stop thinking about my parents. They've tried to protect me from situations like this my whole life. Every call my parents made wondering where I was, every talk they gave me about how the world wasn't always a nice place, everything just came rushing back to me. Whenever I went out alone, they would ask me to call and let them know that I reached safely. And I forgot every single time. So they would call me numerous times. And I would get super-irritated. "Relax, *ma*. Stop being so paranoid. Nothing is going to happen to me," I'd say confidently. Today, I wasn't so sure that nothing would happen to me.'

'Shit. I feel terrible, Tia. I'm an absolute idiot. I guess we're all so used to thinking Canada is safe that we don't realize that anything can happen anywhere. I'm so sorry you went through that tonight,' Zaid replied.

'No, it's okay, Zaid. I think I was meant to experience this. I don't think I would ever have realized how much I owe my parents if I hadn't. First, watching Leigh and her parents together and now this, clearly the cosmos is trying to convey something to me. Something that my pig-headed brain refused to acknowledge earlier. My parents are the only people in the world who would do anything for me. No one else cares about me as much as they do.

And I've been such a bitch to them. All because their love and concern for me made them overreact one day.'

Zaid's forehead furrowed in confusion and Tia realized he had no idea what she was talking about. She hadn't told him about 'the incident'. She actually hadn't told anyone because she had been too embarrassed to talk about it.

Tia hesitated for a moment, and then narrated the whole sorry tale to Zaid about the slapping that had prompted her to come to Canada. He listened quietly and then said, 'Well, my dad left when I was ten. He fell in love with my best friend's mother. He left my mum and me and started living with her. And I couldn't help but feel like it was all my fault. If I hadn't become friends with Althea, our parents would never have met. My dad would never have thought that she was 'the one' and abandoned us. But do you know what the worst part about it all was? I lost my best friend too. My parents got divorced and I didn't even have my best friend's shoulder to cry on. He deprived me of that as well. I couldn't be friends with her anymore. Not now that we shared a father. My mum has been my everything since my dad left. So, trust me, your dad slapping you because he was concerned about you, is not the worst thing a dad can do. I would choose a hundred slaps over hearing my mum cry in her room alone at night and not knowing how to comfort her. We all have issues with our parents but trust me, what you have is a non-issue.'

Tia nodded. She imagined what it was like to be in Zaid's shoes. His childhood must have been really tough.

Yet, looking at him, you would never be able to tell that he was carrying all that pain inside of him. In fact, everyone on campus looked so happy. It wasn't until you had a heart-to-heart with someone that you realized what they had been through. She wondered how many kids on campus came from broken homes. And how many students hid pain and heartache behind their cheery smiles.

'Hey, sleepyhead! Wakey, wakey!' Armaan's voice boomed from her phone.

'Oi. Why're you yelling? It's only 7.00 a.m.,' Tia replied groggily.

'It's okay. You can go back to sleep later, but you have to talk to me now.'

Tia sat up in bed. 'What's with all the enthu at this ungodly hour, A-man?'

'Can't a guy be happy for no reason?'

'Anyone else maybe. Not you. I know you too well. You're basically like this serious uncle at heart,' Tia said.

Armaan laughed. 'Gee, thanks. But if you have to know, the reason I'm happy is that Rishab is getting married! And it's a Goa wedding, baby!'

'Oh, my God! That is huge! Congrats! Aunty and uncle must be so excited. Give me all the deets, hello! Who is she? How did they meet?' Armaan's older brother was finally getting married!

'Her name is Meghna. She was his friend from college. They knew each other for years but it was pretty platonic. And then one fine day, something changed between them, I guess,' Armaan said.

She really didn't know what to say to that. Was she imagining it or did his tone change when he said the last bit? Was he trying to hint at their relationship? No, come on, don't be silly. Don't read into things.

'So, when's the big day?' she quickly steered the conversation.

'Fifteenth Jan! I haven't told Neha and Stan yet. It all got finalized today and you're the first person I've told. Neha and Stan are going to be super excited; they've wanted to do a Goa trip for a while now. And now, we have the perfect excuse. You know you have to be there, right?'

'Ah! But my winter semester will start by then! Crap! Crap! Crap! Man, I really, really want to be at Rishab's wedding.'

'Then make it happen! Come on! It's Goa! Neha, Stan, you and me! Can you imagine how awesome it'll be? Hey, that rhymed! I'm a poet, and I didn't even know it,' he laughed.

Wow, Armaan must really be in a good mood if he's cracking silly jokes. 'Okay, stop tempting me. I'll see what I can do,' she replied.

'That's my girl! So how was the weekend? Anything exciting happen?'

'Oh, you have *no* idea!' She filled him in on the fabulous time she had in Toronto followed by her scary wait alone in the dark road at midnight experience.

Armaan was not amused. 'Oh, my God! That's really scary. You should be more careful, Ti. Thank God, you're okay. That could have turned out to be really bad. This Zaid dude is so irresponsible.'

Tia laughed. 'Naw, he's not. His phone died! It could have happened to anyone. And I'm fine. I did freak out a bit last night, but now I'm totally fine. Zaid is pretty cool, actually. We've bonded recently. My talk with him made me realize how lucky I am to have my parents. He helped me get over my issues with Ma and Pa.'

'What issues?' Armaan asked.

She realized that she hadn't told Armaan about what happened with her parents all those months ago. She filled him in on the events of that fateful night and he fell silent.

'Hello? Say something,' she said.

'I was with you that night. So much happened and you didn't think to tell me,' he said quietly.

'But I didn't tell anyone about it. I didn't even tell Nene. I was too embarrassed at the time. And I was frustrated with my parents. I just wanted to get away.'

'But you could have told me about it once you got to Canada. You told this Zaid about it, didn't you?'

'Yeah, but only because I was so overwhelmed by the "almost incident" last night. And I was so emotional after seeing Leigh with her parents. He was in front of me; it all just came out...'

'Well, it's not my fault I'm not in front of you. You're the one who chose to run away instead of confronting the situation at home. And by the way, in case you hadn't noticed, it's not 1940. I'm literally a WhatsApp message or Facetime call away. So, this whole "distance" thing is a load of crap. I don't let the distance between us affect anything. You're the first person I told about Rishab's wedding. I could have told Nene or Stan because they were "in front of me", but I didn't. Just about anyone won't do for me. But clearly you don't feel that way. In your mind, there's absolutely no difference between a random guy you've just met and me. Thanks, *haan*. Good to know.'

What? What was Armaan on about? Why was he getting so touchy about this?

'Armaan, what are you saying? It isn't like that and you know it. You're really important to me. Zaid is a friend, but he's nowhere close to what you and I have. You're one of my best friends! But you can't get upset about me not telling you about this thing with my parents. It wasn't about you. It was about me feeling stifled at home. I didn't want to talk about it then. I've forgiven my parents for it but I barely want to talk about it now. It's still a sensitive topic for me and I'm uncomfortable talking about it.'

'Then I won't make you any more uncomfortable. You can go back to sleep now. Sorry I disturbed you,' Armaan said. He hung up.

Tia stared at her phone baffled. What the hell had gotten into Armaan?

His phone rang and he picked it up on the first ring.

'Hey, what's up?' Rachna's voice on the phone sounded excited.

'Hey, uh, not much. You tell me?' Zaid replied.

'I got my assignment back! The one we stayed up for all night. Guess what? I got an "A"! And I owe it all to you. So, I wanted to invite you for dinner tonight? My treat?'

'Hey, that's awesome! So happy to hear that our efforts

paid off. I would love to do dinner but ... um ... tonight looks a little difficult. Can we do this another time?' Zaid tried to match her enthusiasm but he sounded a little distracted.

She knew it was unreasonable to expect him to be free every time she called him, but she couldn't help but feel a little bummed that he wasn't available tonight.

She hung up and decided to call Precious. No reason why she shouldn't celebrate tonight, anyway. As luck would have it, Precious had a test the next day and couldn't head out.

Rachna lay on her bed and stared at the ceiling. She hated when this happened. She was all set to celebrate and she had no one to go out with. It was at times like these when she really missed home. As much as she was having a good time and had made good friends, there were still days when she felt completely alone. She decided to catch up on her favourite TV shows. The one good thing about being in Canada was that the TV shows aired at the same time they did in the US.

She went down to the lounge in the building and sure enough, a group of students had gathered around to watch the latest episode of *How to Get Away with Murder*. She found a couch and settled in.

The minute the episode started, she found herself gripped by the show. She forgot all her worries and was sucked into the world of Annalise Keating.

Fiona lay in bed and scrolled through Facebook. Her phone rang. It was Karan. She knew she should answer it but she simply wasn't up to speaking with Karan. She was being unfair by ignoring his calls but couldn't bring herself to talk to him. She couldn't really bring herself to talk to anyone, for that matter. She felt listless; all she wanted to do was to burrow under her duvet and hide away from the world. Her phone beeped to let her know that she had a new voice message. It would probably be Karan asking her why she had gone MIA and telling her to call him back because he missed hearing her voice. She pressed 1 to hear it. Sure enough, Karan's voice boomed through the phone.

'Hey, Fiona, where are you? I've been calling, but there's been no response from you. I didn't want to do it this way, but I can't keep this from you anymore. I ... uh ... I think we should break up. It's hard keeping a long-distance relationship going. We hardly talk anymore. I feel like you're happier being alone. And the other thing is ... I've met someone. I don't know how it started but I really like Niti. I haven't done anything about it. You and I had decided that we would tell each other if we met someone so I'm honouring our agreement. I never meant to hurt you, Fi. You will always be special to me. We've had way too many good times for things to end bitterly between us. You're also the coolest, most practical girl I've ever met so I know you're not going to overreact ...'

The voice message ended abruptly. No wonder Karan had been trying to call her so frantically for the last few days. At first, she couldn't believe what she had just heard. Karan, who was head over heels in love with her, who had begged her to not break up with him before she left

India, had just broken up with her. Before she knew what was happening, she began tearing up. Soon, she was full-blown sobbing. She had never felt this alone in her entire life. She couldn't even describe how she felt. She felt guilty for sure; Karan had had the decency to tell her that he liked someone else before acting on it. Unlike her; she had hooked up with Arjun and hadn't even considered Karan's feelings. And yes, she had probably fallen out of love with Karan – why else would she be so drawn to Arjun – but the one thing she had counted on was the perpetuity of Karan's love for her. It was selfish, but it was what it was. And now, Karan was going to be happy with a new girlfriend and she was going to be alone. She was broken. And she truly believed she was never going to get fixed. She replayed the events of the last few days and they seemed surreal. She had to remind herself that none of it was a bad dream. It was all very real; it had all happened. In just a few days, her simple easy-going life had turned topsy-turvy.

She remembered the day it all started. She woke up a week ago feeling nauseous. She thought she must have eaten something dicey the previous day and didn't give it too much thought. The next morning she was completely fine. However, four hours down the line, when she was sitting in class, she was overcome by the urge to throw up. She excused herself from class and ran to the nearest washroom, where she proceeded to puke for the next five minutes.

She went straight to the doctor on campus. She expected him to say she had got food poisoning, but instead he asked her, 'Have you been using protection? You might be pregnant.'

Her heart beat wildly. She felt the blood drain from her cheeks. No way! She couldn't be pregnant. Could she? Her parents' faces swam in front of her eyes. She didn't even want to think about how they would react if it turned out to be true. When was her last period? She remembered that she had had her period on Nat's birthday which was on 15th September. It was the 20th of October that day. She generally had a very regular period cycle. How had she not noticed that she was late?

'I suggest you get a pregnancy urine test done. You'll get it at any pharmacy. I'm also prescribing a blood test to make doubly sure. Don't get stressed out. Take the tests first and we'll figure out our options post that, okay?' the doctor said kindly.

She wondered how many girls he said this to everyday. That explained how nonchalant he was. But this was a huge deal to her. When she saw teenagers pregnant on TV shows and movies, she empathized but never in her wildest dreams did she think she would one day be in their shoes. She thanked the doctor and walked out of his office in a daze.

She went for the blood test first. She was told that the results would be sent to Dr Ronson the next day. Although the blood test was the most accurate pregnancy test, she decided to take the home pregnancy urine test too. The next day was too far away and she couldn't wait that long to find out if her life had changed forever or not.

When she got to the pharmacy, she murmured to the pharmacist, 'One pregnancy test.'

'Sorry, can you repeat that?' the young girl demanded loudly.

She felt as if all the customers in the store were staring at her.

She repeated herself, louder this time.

'Which test do you want? We have Easy@home, Clearblue, One Step Early Pregnancy test.'

'Uh. I don't know. The most popular brand?'

'That would be Easy@home, then. Think you might be pregnant, huh? Best of luck, yeah. I have a friend who has been trying for two years now. Poor girl buys these kits all the time and then it turns out to be negative,' the chatty pharmacist continued.

She prayed really hard that she was in that girl's shoes right now. She'd do anything for the test to be negative. 'Right. Uh. How much is this?'

She paid the pharmacist fifteen dollars and walked out of the pharmacy. She raced back to her apartment.

She was greeted by Nat when she entered the flat.

'Hey! Where have you been? I'm starving. I was just going to get a sandwich. Coming?'

'Uh, no. I really need to poop. You carry on,' she replied.

Nat laughed. 'You want something?'

Yes, I desperately want to not be pregnant.

'No, I'm fine,' Fiona said.

She entered the bathroom and took a deep breath. This was it. The moment of truth was finally here. She sat on the toilet seat and peed on the stick. The five minutes that she waited for the result were the longest five minutes of her life. She read the instructions on the box over and over as she waited for the results. The box said the strip would have one line if you're not pregnant and two lines if you are. She stared at her watch and counted the minutes as they ticked by. When the five minutes were up, she hesitantly looked at the strip.

There were two distinct blue lines. Fuck. Fuck. Fuck. Shit. Shit. Shit. No way. Oh, my God! No. No, God, no. Why was this happening to her? What would she do now? Her heartbeat quickened for the second time that day. Any chance the test was wrong? Yes, of course it could be wrong. That was it. She would wait until the next day for the blood test results before she freaked out. At that moment, what she needed the most was to stay calm. Of course, that was easier said than done.

She went to her room, sat on her bed and grabbed her laptop. She googled 'abortion in Canada' and began reading all about it. She found out that she could either have a surgical or medical abortion. With surgery, the process was completed in one shot with less bleeding after the procedure than medical or non-surgical abortion. She was in the middle of reading an article on the advantages and disadvantages of both methods, when Nat walked into her room.

'What are you doing?' she asked, munching on chips.

Fiona jumped. 'Ah! You scared me. I, um, nothing, just doing some research for an assignment.'

'I met Arjun at the food court. He has downloaded

some new movies and asked us to come chill and watch movies in his room. I'm done with my work and studying for the day. What about you?'

Arjun. He was the reason she was in this mess. She realized she would have to tell him all about it. Her stomach did an uncomfortable belly flop.

'Uh ... no, man. I'm kinda swamped today. I'm going to have to be locked up in my room studying. You go chill at his,' she said.

Ordinarily, she would never have passed up an opportunity to spend time with Arjun. But she couldn't possibly see him and act like everything was normal. She was barely managing to lie to Nat. She needed some alone time to weigh her options.

When Nat left, she spent another two hours reading up on teenage pregnancies and abortions. She found stories of women who had been in the same boat and reading their experiences made her feel a little less alone.

She had no idea when she fell asleep but she woke up to find her head resting on her laptop and her keypad covered with drool. She switched on the light; it was 1.00 a.m. She wondered whether Nat was back from Arjun's place. She could just go to her room and check, but, if Nat was there, she would have to talk to her and she still didn't feel like talking to anyone. She would only feel better once she got the blood test results. But if the blood test confirmed what she suspected was true what would happen next? She would have to get an abortion – no two ways about that. But did she have to tell Arjun? How would he react?

She thought back to how it all started with Arjun. They were all at Van Gogh's one Saturday night last month. Arjun had always been flirtatious towards her, but that night they had both been drinking Jägermeister shots. She didn't even know how much she had had to drink, but, before she knew it, Arjun and she began dancing together. He had pressed his body against hers and she remembered being oh so horny. When his lips met hers, she couldn't believe what a good kisser he was. She had enjoyed kissing Karan of course, but this was something else. She couldn't stop kissing him. She wanted to have sex with him that very night but they were out with a group of friends and they ended up just playing board games with everyone back at Arjun's apartment.

She had woken up with a terrible hangover the next day that resulted in her spending the entire afternoon in bed. She planned staying put in her room, but that was until she got a message from Arjun at 6.00 p.m. that day. It read: 'Hey, Princess Fiona. How are you feeling now? I had an amazing time last night. We could continue where we left off if you're up to it? ;)'

Her heart beat wildly when she read the message. She knew she should think rationally before replying. After all, she was still dating Karan. But her heart and head were relaying two completely different messages. And she ended up listening to her heart. She replied to Arjun's message within ten minutes of receiving it. 'Hey. I had a great time last night too. Feel like crap now, but I guess you could try and make me feel better? ;)'

She read her response over and over again after she

sent it. She watched her phone as it refused to beep back. Shit. Had she come on too strong? She should have played hard-to-get. Damn it.

Twenty minutes later, her phone beeped.

'Outside your flat. Don't want to knock in case Nat or one of your roomies see me ... open the door? ;)'

Woah! She woke up with a jerk. He was outside. Arjun was outside her flat. This was it. She knew what was going to happen next. So how did she feel? Guilty? Nervous? The answer was excited. She opened her door carefully so as to avoid making any noise. The flat was quiet. Everyone was probably nursing hangovers. She ran to the main door and opened it. Arjun stood there, smiling.

'Hey,' she whispered.

'Hey,' he whispered back.

She led him to her room and shut the door.

'So,' she could feel the blood rush to her cheeks.

'So,' he continued.

'Um, I'll be back in ten minutes.' She realized she hadn't brushed her teeth or washed her face. When she saw her reflection in the bathroom mirror, she recoiled in horror. Her mascara and kohl had smudged and she looked like a Goth teenager (and definitely not in a good way). She tried her best to look 'fresh' and not like a car had run over her. Ten minutes later, she looked only marginally less like a homeless person, but this was the best she could do and so she returned to her room.

He was sitting on her bed. When she entered the room, he pulled her close to him. He clearly didn't want to waste any time. His lips met hers. His kiss was gentle at first but then it became hungrier. She found herself responding with the same passion. His hand found its way under her T-shirt. He smiled when he realized she hadn't worn a bra. Within seconds, he had peeled it off. His lips made their way from her neck to her breasts. He licked, sucked and bit her until she could take no more. She pulled his T-shirt off. He had rock solid abs. Ah! Delicious!

It was her turn to savour his body. She licked his body from his chest down to his waist. She unbuttoned his jeans and felt his bulge. He moaned. Suddenly, he turned her over and kissed her all over her body. He pulled her PJs down and kissed her thighs. He teased her for a while by kissing her everywhere except where she wanted him to kiss her. When he finally did venture there, she moaned in pleasure. 'Deeper, deeper. There, right there. Stay there. Oh, my God!'

He took out a condom from the pocket of his jeans that lay abandoned on the bed, and put it on.

When he entered her, she struggled to keep her voice low as she moaned. He stared into her eyes as he moved in and out of her. He moved faster until they climaxed together. He rolled off her and they lay next to each other panting. She sighed contentedly. 'That was amazing!' she told him.

'I know. Hangover cured?' he teased.

There was a sudden knock on her room door.

'Fi? What's up? Open up! Let's eat. I'm starving!' It was Nat.

Shit. She didn't want Nat to see Arjun in her bed. She

started panicking. What could she say to Nat to get her off her back? She looked at Arjun helplessly. He gestured for her to stay calm by nodding and putting his right hand up. He kinda looked like mute Munni from *Bajrangi Bhaijaan* doing that. She suddenly had the urge to giggle. This was insane. It felt like she was hiding a boy in her room from her parents. Wasn't the whole point of living on campus that she had the freedom to do whatever (or whoever) she wanted? She decided that it was okay if Nat found out. What was the big deal anyway? Arjun was now doing a silent cough. He raised his eyebrows at Fiona. What? Was he feeling sick? Oh! He was trying to tell her that she could pretend to be sick.

'Nat! I'm feeling super sick. I can't move. You go eat. I just want to sleep,' she croaked.

'Yeah, you drank like seven shots yesterday! And I hope you remember that you totally made out with Arjun! But okay, cool, rest it out. Let me know when you're up to eating or whatever,' she said.

She heard Nat's footsteps recede and the main door slam shut. Nat must have gone over to the food court.

She whispered to Arjun. 'That was close. So, what now?'

'Now, *I'm* starving. And I don't intend to hide in your room all night. Let's wait for like ten minutes or so and then, I'll go back to my room. What's your schedule like tomorrow? Want to come over to mine tomorrow evening?'

'Yeah, my last class is at three tomorrow, so I'm free in the evening.' She nodded. She couldn't help but feel a little disappointed though. Arjun could have asked her to go out and eat with him tonight. Her brain told her that Arjun probably didn't ask her that because she would get caught if Nat saw her come back from a restaurant. But still. He could have at least offered. There was something else niggling at her. He didn't actually tell her that he liked her. Although she had a massive crush on him, he was rather non-vocal about his feelings. She told herself that she was reading too much into it and decided to let it go.

The next day, she went to his place, as decided, and they had fabulous sex again. This time she was on top. They continued their 'secret' liaison for the next few weeks. But over time, their friends and roommates found out. Zaid saw her leave Arjun's apartment one day. Two weeks after they had started hooking up, Nat found out too. She saw Arjun sneak out of Fiona's room. 'Oh, my God! You naughty girl! I thought the two of you just make out at clubs when you're drunk! I didn't know you were doing it! Why would you hide this from me? What the hell? I want all the details! Spill!' When she filled her in, Nat was cool about the whole thing. One of the reasons Fiona had been hesitant to tell Nat was that she thought Nat had a crush on Arjun too. But seeing how normal Nat was after finding out about Arjun and her, Fiona wasn't so sure that Nat had ever had a crush on Arjun.

And so, she had been hooking up with Arjun for the last five weeks. They used condoms the entire time. Which is why she couldn't understand how this had happened. She knew there were rare cases where condoms weren't effective, but why did that have to happen in her case? Unless, Arjun had been so drunk one of the times that he hadn't worn the condom properly. Or was it that time she was so drunk, she didn't even notice if he was wearing a condom to begin with? Or maybe the condom had expired? No one thinks to check these things in the throes of passion. Or maybe they had been so horny and drunk that they hadn't noticed when a condom tore. She could speculate as much as she wanted, but she would never really know what had gone wrong now. Arghhhhh! 'Abstinence is the best form of prevention.' All of a sudden, her School Guidance teacher's words popped in her head. Fuck. This was so fucking unfair. Most of the kids on campus were having sex and nothing happened to them. Why did she have to be the unlucky one?

She got out of bed and grabbed a packet of Skittles from her bookshelf. She opened the packet and climbed back into bed. She stuffed her mouth with a handful of Skittles and stared blankly at the wall in front of her. Her mind wandered back to the previous week again. When she had gone back to Dr Ronson for her blood test results, he confirmed that she was indeed pregnant. When she told him that she definitely wanted an abortion, he told her that she would have to get one at a clinic downtown. 'Luckily, your international student health insurance will cover the expenses of the surgery,' Dr Ronson told her.

Lucky indeed, she thought bitterly.

He called the clinic to schedule an appointment for her. 'Friday noon, okay for you? You're going to need someone to come with you. You'll be drowsy after surgery; you'll need someone to bring you back,' Dr Ronson said matter-of-factly.

'The surgery will be done in twenty minutes. You'll be able to do all your regular activities from Saturday itself. Of course, there will be bleeding, which may last for up to a week. So, you can think of it as a normal period. You'll have to go for a check-up next week, just to make sure everything is okay.' He looked deep into her eyes and said, 'You'll be okay. Trust me.'

She nodded. She didn't care if he said the same thing to all the teenage pregnant women whom he met. She definitely felt better. So she needed someone to go with her on Friday. She had to tell Arjun about all of this. She hadn't seen him since Sunday and surprisingly, she hadn't heard from him since then either. He usually messaged her every second day, if not every day. She dialled his number as soon as she left Health Services, but it was switched off. He must have forgotten to charge his phone again. She knew his class schedule as well as she did her own, courtesy of fooling around for the last few weeks. It was a Wednesday which meant his first class was at 1.00 p.m. It was only 11.30 a.m. then, which meant he would be at his apartment. She walked to his res. His apartment door was open; one of his flat mates must have forgotten to shut it. She entered the apartment and headed towards his room. She knocked on his door.

'Who is it?' Arjun hollered.

Brian, his roommate, popped out of the adjoining room at that moment. He waved at Fiona. He knew her pretty well by now.

'It's me, Brian. Open up, I have something important to tell you,' Brian yelled.

She heard Arjun's heavy footsteps as he walked to his door.

He semi-opened the door. His hair was dishevelled. He wasn't wearing a shirt; just his jeans. 'What's up?' he scowled enquiringly at Brian. When he saw Fiona, his expression changed.

'Oh, Fiona! What are you doing here?'

Brian said, 'She misses you, obviously! Okay, I'm outta here. Later, guys.' Brian walked out of the apartment.

'I need to talk to you about something really important, Arjun. I called, but your phone was switched off. Anyway, can I come in?' Fiona asked.

'Uh, yeah ... but I'm late for class. Why don't I put on my T-shirt and then we can walk towards my class and talk?' he replied. He was still blocking the entrance to his room.

A flicker of realization crossed Fiona's face. She pushed him aside and entered his room. Sure enough, he had company. Sitting in his bed, cheeks flushed and with the duvet pulled up to cover her assets, was Nat.

'Oh, my God,' Fiona exclaimed. She couldn't believe this was happening.

'Fiona, I can explain. Arjun kissed me when I came over here yesterday. I pushed him away because of you, but he insisted that you guys were not exclusive. You're just friends with benefits, who are allowed to date and sleep with other people, right? I mean, you have a boyfriend back in India whom you claim to love.'

Fiona was at a loss for words. She couldn't explain how she felt towards Arjun and Nat. And they didn't deserve to know. She walked out of Arjun's room. She couldn't stand being in his apartment building anymore. The elevator would take another five minutes and she didn't have that kind of time. She ran all the way down the stairs from the sixth floor. When she was finally outside, she took a deep breath. What the fuck was happening in her life? Why had her easy going, happy life taken such a melodramatic turn? She couldn't help feeling like she was in the throes of a really bad nightmare; she fervently hoped that that was all it was, a horrible dream; and that she would wake up any minute now. She would go mad if she didn't talk to someone about this. But who? The only person she could think of was Zaid. She dialled his number. She didn't even realize it had happened, but her eyes had filled with tears.

'Hello,' she said in a choked voice.

'Hey? What's wrong? Are you crying?' Zaid asked, concerned. When she remained silent, he continued. 'Don't cry. It will be okay.'

'I'm ... uh ... can we meet? Can I come to your apartment?' she sniffled.

'Yes, I'll be at mine in five minutes ... come over.' Zaid sounded worried.

When she reached his place, he had a glass of water waiting for her. She sipped the water and attempted to collect herself. They sat on his bed.

'What happened, Fi?' Zaid asked.

She didn't even know where to begin. 'I ... I just found out I'm pregnant,' she said at last.

Zaid's jaw dropped. 'Oh, shit. I mean, are you sure?'

'Yes, I'm sure. This isn't even the half of it. I went over to Arjun's place to tell him about it because, obviously ... um ... it's his ... but when I got there, I saw him in bed with Nat.'

'Oh, fuck.' Zaid looked genuinely lost for words. 'That's ... I don't even know what to say,' he said finally.

'I know. Even I don't know what I'm feeling now. Like death, of course. But also, really, really, *reallllllllly* angry. Like I want to smash something. I mean ... fuck ... can you imagine?'

Zaid put his arm around her and drew her into a hug.

'I actually do know exactly how you feel. I was in the same situation not too long ago,' he said.

'What ... you got pregnant too?' she chuckled through her tears.

He smiled. 'Okay, not that part, of course. But I did catch my girlfriend of two years cheating on me. Walked in on her with this guy. I felt angry, sad, stupid, worthless ... you name it. It took me a while, but I finally did bounce back. I know it feels like your life is over right now. But trust me Fi, it isn't.'

She let the tears roll. 'I'm so mad at Arjun and Nat. But I'm also so mad at myself. I just ... I fell for the wrong guy. Arjun clearly doesn't care about me. And he never did. At least yours was an ex. She must have loved you at some point. What is Arjun to me? What did we even have? I fell hard for him. I had such a bad crush, I couldn't even ask him how he really felt about me. He kissed me one night and I was over the moon. And then when we had sex, it felt so good, I didn't want it to stop. I guess, if I'm honest with myself, on some level I knew he didn't really like me that way. But I stayed in denial. And now, now look at me. I'm frikkin' pregnant. What have I done? I guess it's ... it's probably karma for cheating on Karan. I'm a slut and this is what sluts get, right?'

'Shh, come on, Fi. Stop it. Stop blaming yourself. It's not your fault you got pregnant. It could happen to anyone.'

She shook her head. 'I should have been more careful. My parents are spending so much money on my education and I'm squandering their hard-earned money. If they find out I'm pregnant, they won't be able to handle it. They'll die.'

'Fiona, calm down. You're just making this worse for yourself. I know you feel guilty, but why don't we focus on the solution instead of the problem. You've met the doctor, right? So, you've decided to have an abortion?' he asked hesitantly.

'Yeah, I have. What other option do I have? So yeah, I've been scheduled for surgery on Friday at noon at the clinic downtown...'

'Okay, good. Well, not, good, but, see, you've taken action. That's the best way to deal with a situation. So, you're ready for the surgery on Friday, right?'

'Yeah, I suppose. I think I probably will feel really

relieved once it's done. The sooner it happens, the sooner I can get all of this out of my mind.'

'Yes, exactly. I agree. You'll feel better after the surgery, for sure. How long is the surgery?'

'Just twenty minutes. But the doctor said I'll be drowsy post-surgery, so I'll need someone to bring me back home.'

'I'll come with you, of course. It's going to be fine, Fi. Everything is going to be okay. You'll see.'

She smiled gratefully at him. 'Thanks, Zaid. I don't know what I would have done if it weren't for you. Ideally, the father of the baby or my best friend should have come with me. But since the two of them are too busy having sex with each other, I really have no one else, except you.'

'And I'm all you need. I'm an amazing friend, hello! Why would you need anyone else?' He tried to cheer her up.

She nodded. 'You really are an amazing friend, Z. Thank you.'

Two days later, she found herself at the clinic with Zaid.

'Fiona?' The doctor came up to her. 'Hi, I'm Dr Adams.'

She tried to speak, but the words wouldn't come out.

'Hi, Dr Adams, this is Fiona. She's a little emotional right now, but she's ready,' Zaid stepped in.

Fiona smiled at Zaid. It was amazing how she could still smile even though she wished she was dead.

The doctor patted her shoulder. Dr Adams was in her mid-forties and had a kind face. Fiona was happy to notice that she looked genuinely kind. She hated doctors who feigned concern.

'Dr Ronson has already filled me in. It's a routine surgery, don't worry. And luckily, you're not that far along in the pregnancy. You'll be fine. It's natural to feel nervous and upset. We have a post-surgery counselling session that you can come in for anytime you like. I'd highly recommend a session. Sometimes, talking to a stranger about how you feel makes all the difference.'

Zaid nodded. 'She'll definitely come for a session. I'll bring her whenever she wants to come.'

Dr Adams smiled. 'Great. So, Fiona, can we get you ready for surgery?'

She took a deep breath. She was still crying, but she felt ready. As ready as she would ever be, in any case. She nodded.

Zaid gave her a tight hug. 'See you when it's over. Stay strong.'

She went through the motions and changed into the hospital gown. A nurse took a blood test. She was then gurneyed into the operation theatre, where she was given local anaesthesia. She started to panic when the doctor started the procedure. This was it. The moment she had dreaded for the last three days was finally here. She felt the same uneasiness she usually felt in the pit of her stomach before an exam. That feeling of, 'there's no going back now. This is really happening.'

The cramps began. She had never had painful period cycles so she wasn't really used to the pain, even though it wasn't as bad as she had imagined it would be. She couldn't help missing her mother. She thought back to all the times that Mom had been by her side when she had been sick through the years. She had been there for every minor cold, flu or food poisoning instance and yet, now, during the scariest moments of her life with the gravest consequences imaginable and when she had needed her the most, Mom wasn't around to hold her hand. What was worse was that her mother didn't even know what she was going through.

Mom had called her yesterday but Fiona had barely spoken to her for five minutes. She had lied to her saying that she had a major test the next day. In a sense, it wasn't a complete lie. The day definitely felt like a test. Except that the impact of this test on her life would be greater than any other.

'And it's done,' Dr Adams announced. 'That wasn't so bad now, was it? Reese here will take you to the recovery room,' Dr Adams said, giving Fiona's hand a quick squeeze.

Dr Adams gently let Fiona's hand go and the nurse, Reese, wheeled her to the recovery room. Fiona was given Tylenol to help control the pain and offered juice and crackers. She hadn't eaten anything since the morning and was happy to finally be able to eat.

There was a hesitant knock on the room door; Zaid entered the room.

'How are you feeling, Fi?'

'I'm okay, I guess. I'm cramping, but I'll be fine,' she croaked.

Dr Adams came into the room again. She handed Fiona a prescription for antibiotics.

'I'll go get them from the pharmacy outside,' Zaid immediately volunteered.

He was back within twenty minutes. Reese told Fiona that she could go home. Well, back to her res. Home felt really far away right now. No matter how much Fiona wished she was at home with her mom to take care of her, she knew that that wasn't possible. Zaid stayed with her for a while. He ordered a pizza for Fiona and left only after she had eaten.

She spent the entire weekend in bed and now that it was Monday, she knew she should head to class as per normal. Except that she couldn't will herself to get out of bed. She lay there like a zombie.

The anaesthesia had long worn off, but she still felt numb.

Rachna emerged from one of the most boring lectures she had been to in ages. Actually, she had been bored all day. She had attended five lectures since morning and had retained nothing. Zilch. Mama and Papa would be so proud. She didn't know what it was. She had just been so out of it and listless all week. Actually, she did know what it was. She didn't know what was going on with Zaid. He had been busy all week. It was like he was avoiding her or something. Typical guy.

She supposed it was her fault for assuming that he liked her. Just because someone stayed up all night to help you with your assignment, it didn't mean that he liked you. Maybe he had nothing better to do that night. Her mistake.

But seriously, it had seemed like he really liked her. And so, she couldn't understand why he was suddenly unavailable.

Men were crazy. When she had hated him, he had been running after her. And now that she had begun to have a crush on him, he was ignoring her. She had felt that Zaid and she had really connected. She thought what they had was above immature mind games but maybe that wasn't the case. Maybe all men really were the same.

She was lost in her own world, thinking these thoughts, when suddenly there he was. Right in front of her. But he wasn't alone. He was with Fiona. Fiona smiled at Zaid and he hugged her. Fiona waved goodbye to him and walked away. God, what was with this girl? She seemed to go after every guy that Rach liked. First, Arjun. And now, Zaid. And of course, there really was no competition because as much as she hated admitting it, Fiona was rather stunning.

Rachna wondered what to do; she knew she should look away, but she was transfixed. And then, suddenly, it was too late. Zaid noticed her staring at him. He waved to her and smiled a huge smile. He seemed genuinely happy to see her. See? It was all so confusing.

'Rach! Hey!' he greeted her as he walked up to her.

'Hey.'

'How are you?' he asked.

'Fine.'

She wanted to act normal and nonchalant but she couldn't. She was annoyed. When he realized that she wouldn't say anything further, he said, 'I know I've been

AWOL, but I've had some stuff going on ... anyway, I've missed you. What are you doing now? Are you free to have coffee?'

She knew she should act pricey. He couldn't just ignore her for a week and then expect them to pick up from where they left off. But she was just so happy to see him. And she really did want to talk to him.

'Yeah, I'm done for the day. Tim Hortons?'

They walked towards the coffee shop.

'Congrats on doing so well on the assignment. I really wanted to celebrate with you when you called me that night but I ... I couldn't.'

She nodded. 'So, have you had lots of assignments this week?'

'A few. The usual,' he said.

They reached the coffee shop and chose to sit at a table by the window. It was actually the same table they sat at when Zaid first opened up to her. She remembered having a really good time that day. Today, however, there was tension between them. It was the void of words unspoken. She wanted to ask him outright why he had disappeared but something told her he didn't want to talk about it. But she couldn't hold it in any longer.

'Why did you disappear, Zaid? If you haven't been extra busy with assignments, then what could it possibly be? Your family doesn't live here. What else was keeping you? And be honest with me. You know I'm a straight shooter. I don't like playing games. And if you ... if you think I'm just some "option" for you, I'm not going to stand for it. You had warned me about Arjun because

I was just an "option" for him. So now please be upfront and tell me if I'm just that for you as well. Or, if you're still hung up on Devina, then just let me know. You can't just ignore me and then show up when you're bored. That's not how … how a true friendship works.'

Zaid took her hand in his. She felt a tingle.

'Rach, it's not like that. It really isn't. I'm not playing games. And you're not an option for me. And what we have is … is … more than friendship. We both know that. I really like you. I didn't think I'd like anyone after Devina. Far from it. But then I met you. I disappeared because a friend needed me. I had to help my friend with something really important. And I'm the only one she has right now. But she's just a friend. You have to trust me.'

He looked earnestly at her and she was lost for words. She was processing everything he just said. He liked her! Correction; he *really* liked her! See, she knew it! She couldn't believe it. But then she thought about what he had said after that. He had a friend; a *girl* friend who needed him right now. He was probably talking about Fiona. But was he screwing Rachna over? Was she one of those gullible girls who easily got taken for a ride by any guy they fancied? When she heard about them or saw them being taken for a ride on TV shows, she wanted to scream: 'Don't be stupid, girlfriend! He is so manipulating you. Stand up for yourself! Grow a spine already!'

'Okay,' she said to him.

'Okay, what?'

'Okay, I trust you. I like you too, Zaid. Obviously, I do.' She smiled at him.

He smiled at her, too. She felt so free now that it was out there; no more confusion. She liked him and he liked her. She couldn't believe it was out there, but it was.

'So,' he said.

'So,' she replied.

'Are we going out?'

'That depends. Are you asking me out?'

'Yesss,' he replied.

'Then, yesss, we're going out,' she beamed.

He leaned over the table and kissed her. The kiss was gentle and sweet. Her heart was thumping wildly. She would have to pinch herself. Just like that, one of the most boring days of her life had turned into the most eventful day ever.

Rachna stood in the wings and took a deep breath.

'I'm going to be okay. All I have to do is walk. Modelling is easy. I am a confident, beautiful woman. The world is my oyster. And in the end, nothing matters,' she tried giving herself a pep talk, but didn't feel calm. How did her mum do it? It was so hard to be 'zen'.

She peeked from behind the curtains and scanned the audience. She couldn't see Zaid anywhere. He hadn't replied to her last message either. She just didn't know what was going on with him.

After he asked her out last week, she obviously thought she would see much more of him.

But he had been busy all week. They had gone on only

two dates that week. And both times, he had seemed preoccupied.

'Hellooooo, everyone! Welcome to the ISA cultural show! We have got an hour of entertaining performances and a fashion show ... Bollywood style! And as you know, we have a super-fun mixer planned for you after this, so make sure you don't go anywhere after the show. So, are you ready to be spellbound?'

Rachna was jolted out of her reverie by the emcee's voice.

Shit. The show was about to begin. Her co-participants queued up behind her.

The audience cheered as the song '*Aao huzoor tumko*' began playing.

The emcee entered the wings and Rachna stepped out on to the stage.

She sashayed to the front of the stage, smiled and pirouetted before swaying back behind the backdrop. She heard the audience cheering and clapping as she vanished into the wings.

'Good job, Rach!' The emcee smiled at her. She smiled back. That wasn't so bad. She had done it! She had been so nervous and the moment was over in the blink of an eye.

She watched as the other participants promenaded on the stage. Now for the next bit. The song changed to '*I'm sexy and I know it*'. This was the grand finale. The pace was much quicker. The choreographer had told all the participants to dance and clap and do whatever came to them as they paraded. 'Just have fun,' she heard the choreographer's voice behind her.

She walked on to the stage with a huge smile plastered on her face. She did a little jig, blew kisses to the audience and clapped. She heard the applause intensify when she blew air kisses and that made her smile some more.

As the models walked off the stage, they heard the thunderous clapping.

She hugged her fellow models and choreographer. 'You guys were awesome! Rach, you supermodel! You were so confident! You go, girl!' the choreographer said.

Rachna beamed. Her heart was thumping with a major adrenaline rush. She couldn't believe she had pulled this off. Modelling was so much fun! She felt like a contestant on America's next top model. All those hours of watching the show had paid off. Tyra Banks had taught her how to 'smize' – smile with her eyes. If only she was tall enough to be a real model. Tiny as she was, she knew she would never get an opportunity like that again. Which was why she had grabbed it when she read the pamphlet for the culture show three weeks ago.

She walked into the audience. There was really only one person with whom she wanted to share her happiness and he was nowhere to be seen. She wondered what he thought about her catwalk. Did he find her 'smize' sexy enough? She walked through the hall looking for Zaid. People smiled at her. Three random people told her she rocked. She smiled. She knew she had done a good job. But she wanted to hear it from his lips.

She finally spotted him at the far end of the fourth row from the front. She tried waving to him but he didn't see her. The seats on either side of him were occupied. He was flanked by Fiona on one side and a girl whom she didn't recognize, on the other.

'Oh, my God, Rach! You were *amazing*! So hot, my friend!' Precious was standing behind her.

She hugged Precious. 'What are you doing standing here? Let's go find seats and watch the rest of the show,' Precious said.

Rachna flicked one last glance in Zaid's direction and went with Precious.

Post the show, everyone headed to a hall in the next building for the mixer. Rachna needed to change into her jeans and so Precious and she went to her room to change.

Half an hour later, they made their way to the mixer. She was greeted by the sound of '*DJ wale babu*' blasting through the speakers as she neared the hall. She walked through the crowd and finally saw Zaid standing in a corner of the room. He was deep in conversation with the girl he had been sitting next to during the show.

He looked up and saw Rachna.

'Baby! Oh, my God! You were amazing up there. I'm so proud of you,' he said, hugging her tight.

'You were really good,' said the girl beside him.

'Rach, this is Tia. She's from my class. Tia, Rach.'

They were joined by Fiona.

'You were great, Rachna.' She smiled.

Rachna smiled back at them.

'Uh, Zaid, sorry to interrupt, but could I talk to you for a second?' Fiona asked.

'I'll be right back, Rach,' Zaid said and accompanied Fiona outside.

Rach wondered what to say to Tia.

'That's a cute top,' she said when she couldn't think of anything.

Tia began talking to Rachna about campus, but Rachna couldn't really pay attention. What was Zaid doing with Fiona? Wasn't Fiona all over Arjun just a few weeks ago? But she had just seen Arjun dancing and whispering into the ear of another girl. Had Fiona moved on from Arjun? And did she now have her sights on Zaid?

About twenty minutes or so later, Zaid returned without Fiona. 'Sorry, guys. That took longer than I expected. Fiona wasn't feeling well, so she had to return to her apartment,' Zaid announced to Tia and Rachna.

He offered to get them drinks and walked off to the bar after noting their drink orders.

The DJ played '*Angrezi beat*' and everyone around her cheered.

Precious was having a fabulous time on the dancefloor. A turbaned guy was showing her bhangra moves and she followed him excitedly. All around her, people were drinking and dancing. Everyone was having a wonderful time, except her. She had started the night on a high, but now she felt this burning sensation in her gut. She recognized the emotion. She was jealous. Zaid had become the Pied Piper overnight and girls were following him blindly. Zaid brought the drinks over to Tia and her.

'Cheers,' Tia said enthusiastically and the three of them clinked their glasses together.

'Come on, ladies! You're the experts. Show me some

bhangra moves!' Zaid said. He was in high spirits, courtesy of three glasses of vodka and coke.

Ordinarily three glasses of wine were enough to get Rachna drunk, but she simply wasn't feeling lightheaded today.

Nonetheless, they went to the dancefloor. Rachna was just beginning to have fun when Arjun and his new arm candy joined them. Zaid's smile faded as soon as Arjun joined the group. He whispered in Rachna's ear, 'Let's go.' He gestured to Tia to join them and the three of them moved to another corner of the room.

Rachna wondered what that was about. She was about to ask Zaid, when Arjun came up to them and asked Zaid to come outside with him. Zaid was reluctant, but he walked out with Arjun. Rachna was super-confused. What on earth was going on?

She was greeted by a few girls from her classes and she spent time talking to them, one eye glued to the door.

Finally, after what seemed like forever, Zaid emerged through the door.

Rachna left the group with whom she was chatting and rushed to Zaid. 'Is everything okay?' she asked.

'No. Everything is messed up actually,' Zaid replied shortly.

'What happened?'

'I ... uh ... I can't tell you, Rach. I promised someone I wouldn't. I'd be a really bad friend if I broke my promise,' he replied.

'What? Why are you being so cryptic? Come on, Z. You know you can tell me anything.'

'I'm sorry, Rach. Things are a little messed up now. I promise I'll fill you in on everything soon. Let's just try and enjoy what's left of this night, okay?' Zaid said softly.

She wanted to know more, but she could tell he wasn't ready to talk. She nodded and they re-joined the gyrating horde on the dancefloor.

A few minutes later, Tia and Rachna's classmates joined them. Rachna sighed. She knew Zaid was upset about something. She wanted to be there for him just like he had been there for her, but he refused to let her in.

Fiona needed to get over herself. She knew she'd been moping and whinging for far too long now. And honestly, if she had been a friend, she would have wanted to avoid herself too. It was amazing how Zaid put up with her. No one should want to be around this much negativity. It was depressing. She knew all of this. And yet, she hated everyone and everything. She went to her classes because she had to, but once they were done, she would run back to her room and hide from the world. Nat had tried to talk to her all week but she had ignored her. It was really hard ignoring someone when you lived in the same tiny apartment, but she had been successful so far. Nat usually tried talking to her through the door when Fiona was hiding in her room, but yesterday Nat had caught her off guard when she was making herself a sandwich in the kitchen.

'Fiona, you have to hear me out. I'm so, so sorry. I honestly don't know how Arjun and I happened. It was a huge mistake. I know you think I'm a bitch for going after the same guy you were sleeping with. But are we really going to let a guy come between us? Okay, so we've both slept with the same guy. Big deal. It's college. We're young. This was bound to happen. Why are you this upset? I mean, it's not like you love the guy, right? You were fooling around with him too. You have a boyfriend back home whom you love. Arjun is just a silly crush, right?'

When Fiona didn't respond, Nat sighed.

'I really am sorry. If I knew how much this thing with Arjun meant to you, I would never have slept with him. But I mean ... I'm not justifying my behaviour ... but he came on to me. So, if you genuinely like him, he's so not worth it. *He* is the sleazeball here. Anyway, I'll be here whenever you're ready to talk.'

Nat walked away and Fiona congratulated herself on her restraint. She had been so tempted to throw her sandwich at Nat. But thankfully she had stopped herself in time. She realized that would have been a bad decision because for one, she was really hungry and would have had to fix herself another sandwich, and two, there was a good chance that Nat would retaliate and kick her ass. Nat was taller and stronger than Fiona. The girl worked out and Fiona had seen her flex her muscles enough to know that messing with her was a bad idea.

Fiona knew that Nat's reasoning was crap; Nat had made it seem like it was all no big deal, just to make herself feel better. Nevertheless, Fiona couldn't help playing Nat's words out in her head. Was she really overreacting? It was true that Nat didn't know the entire story. She didn't know that Fiona had gotten pregnant and had to have an abortion. She was unaware that Fiona went for a counselling session where she cried for two solid hours.

So, she didn't know what she was talking about for sure. But ... and here was the clincher – did Fiona really love Arjun? And when did she stop loving Karan? And now that Karan had found love again, was she upset because she missed him or was she upset because he was happy and she wasn't?

But, and this was really the most important question – if she did find the answers to her questions, what would be the point? Would she stop feeling like shit?

Oh, and Arjun had still not tried calling her even once post her walking in on him with Nat. She knew he didn't love her, but his not-calling-even-once made her realize that he didn't care, not even a little bit.

She didn't want to think about Arjun though, because if she did, she would have to think about all the times they had sex and then she would think about how she got pregnant. And how she had to get an abortion. How her life as she knew it was over. And how she wished she had never met Arjun and he had never ruined her life.

'Ooh, Josh has just replied!' Leigh squealed.

Tia, who was perched on the bed, grabbed Leigh's phone to read the message. Leigh's roommate Anika rose from her chair and joined Tia on the bed to read the message as well.

'You sound like you have the insider's guide on

Toronto. When are you showing me around?' Tia read the message out loud.

'Oooh, he is so into you! He wants you to show him around Toronto. You have to do it! This weekend!' Tia said, excitedly.

'What! No! I can't seem too eager and available. We should do this next weekend,' Leigh replied.

'Leigh! No! Next weekend is too far away,' Anika protested.

Leigh's gaze shifted from Anika to Tia in confusion.

'Leigh, you really like Josh, right? He is the only guy you've really liked since Peter. So, don't overthink it. Go for it. Show him you're interested. Now let's reply to him,' Tia reasoned.

Tia started typing on Leigh's phone. When she was done typing, Leigh read it and nodded. They showed the message to Anika who also approved it and then Tia hit 'send'. Tia was quite proud of her texting skills. The message she typed back read, 'Oh, I do! I'm extremely cool! Of course, I'm very busy on account of my coolness, but I'll squeeze you into my busy calendar ... this Saturday?'

The phone beeped almost immediately and the girls read Josh's response. He had agreed to the weekend day trip to Toronto. Leigh hugged Anika and Tia excitedly. The three of them jumped up together. 'Yes! Now I need to figure out what to wear, guys!'

Tia smiled. She was really happy for Leigh. She was also amused that she was playing the same role here as she did back in Mumbai. She would listen to all of

Neha's love-life woes and write messages to her various paramours too.

Considering she was such an expert on flirting and messaging, it was a pity that she was still single. Back when she was in Mumbai, she blamed her conservative parents for the dearth of romance in her life. But now that she was in Canada with no restrictions and all the freedom in the world, why the hell was she still on her own? Last week, at a party, Leigh introduced her to a guy from her class. His name was Rishaad. He was pretty decent looking and Tia could picture herself dating him. He took her out for lunch downtown and she seriously thought the date had potential. But this was *her* life, so of course he turned out to be a weirdo. About fifteen minutes into the date, Rishaad started asking her about her skincare regime. She thought that was a little strange, but then she figured that maybe that was his way of getting to know her better. So, she answered his questions about the products she used for her hair and face. And then he got right to it. He was an Amway distributor! He was trying to sell her Amway products on their 'date'. And he tried really hard to get her to become a distributor, too. When she got back to campus an hour later, Leigh and she had a good laugh over the ludicrosity of it all.

But she was beginning to get really irritated. It wasn't like her sole purpose in coming to Canada was to meet 'the one' or anything. However, she did think she would at least meet some interesting guys.

The phone beeped again and both Anika and she

looked at Leigh expectantly. But it was not Leigh's phone that had beeped; it was Tia's. No one (including Tia) was interested in the message she had received because there was no way it was going to be exciting. She clicked on the WhatsApp icon on her phone; she had just got a message from Armaan.

After their 'fight', or rather after the day that Armaan had acted like a spoilt baby, he hadn't spoken to Tia. And that was five days ago. She didn't want to message him because she totally thought he overreacted. But then she really, really missed talking to him. So, she finally messaged him that morning; it was night back in India and he was obviously sleeping.

Her message to him simply read: 'Hey. I miss you. Can we please be friends again?'

His message read: 'No. We can't be friends.'

What the fuck had gotten into him? Why the hell was he so upset? She noticed that he was online and she replied to him immediately.

'Wtf, Armaan! Why are you being so dramatic? You're seriously going to end our friendship because I shared something about my life with a friend here and not with you? Really?!'

She hit 'send' and saw that he had written another message.

'We can't be friends because I want more. I know it sounds all *filmi* and clichéd, but sometimes what you're looking for is right in front of you. It took your moving to Canada for me to see it, but, what can I say, I'm a little slow sometimes ... What I'm trying to say is that I really like you, Tia. And I think you really like me too.'

She read his message and then re-read it. Armaan liked her. Wow. She had always just seen him as a good friend. And because she knew he had the hots for Neha, she never really thought about him that way. However, ever since she moved to Canada, she had gotten used to talking to him all the time. It was so strange that despite him being more than seven thousand miles away, she had never felt this close to him.

She was lost in her thoughts when she saw an incoming Facetime call from him. She turned around to see Leigh holding up dresses while Anika evaluated the outfits.

'Leigh, I'm getting a call from my mum. I'll see you guys later. Bye,' she said and rushed off.

She answered the call as soon as she was in the hallway.

'Hi,' she smiled.

'Hi. Sorry I went AWOL. I know I overreacted when we spoke on Monday. I was just trying to figure out why I felt so bad that you're so close to this Zaid guy. I realized I want to be the first to know everything that's happening in your life. And then it hit me. The reason I told you about bhai's wedding first, the reason I have the need to talk to you all the time, the reason I miss you so much, the reason I hate seeing you cry is that I like you. Like really, really like you, Tia.'

She felt her heart pounding. 'I can't ... I can't believe we're having this conversation. I was always on "Team Neha and Armaan". I honestly thought you guys would end up together. And I know how you've always felt about her—'

'That's done. I'm over Neha,' Armaan interrupted.

She looked at him for a moment. 'Are you sure, Armaan? Is this some rebound thing? Doesn't it bother you when you think about Neha with Varun?'

He looked her straight in the eye (well ... through the camera, but still) and said without hesitation, 'I am completely over Neha. Honestly, there is nothing to be "over". It was a silly crush I've had all these years. But what I have with you, and what we can have, is so, so real, Tia. I feel incomplete when I don't talk to you. I tell you stuff I haven't told anyone. And I guess we've always clicked, but I was just too blinded by my crush on Neha to ever see it. Trust me.'

She smiled, but she was genuinely taken aback by his revelation. She had always thought of Armaan as a really good friend. Did she *like* him or did she like him as a friend? What would it be like to date Armaan? But *whoa*. How could they even date? They lived on different continents now.

He noticed the change in her expression.

'What's wrong?' he asked.

'What's wrong is that you're in India and I'm in Canada. Why couldn't we have fallen in ...' She stopped herself from saying the word 'love'. 'Why couldn't we have liked each other when I was in Bombay? I'm here for another two years. How is this going to work?'

'As you know, I have a track record for liking people and not doing anything about it for years! I'm nothing if not patient. We'll make it work, Tia. I have no doubt about it. And I'm seeing you in Goa in Jan. I have no doubt about that too.'

She had never seen Armaan look so self-assured before. She loved this side of him.

'Armaan, I really like you. Of course, I do. But I've always thought of you as my friend. I'm just … it's just … this is all too sudden. I don't know what to say right now …'

'It's okay, Ti. I get that you're surprised. Why don't you think about it? And Jan isn't too far away. Tell me your decision when we meet in Goa, okay? And until then, I promise I won't bring it up when I talk to you.'

She smiled at him. 'Thanks, Armaan for being so understanding. And I can't wait until Goa.'

'Okay, we're going to leave in ten minutes. I'm going to do a roll call – say "yes" when you hear your name: "Andrew!"' the volunteer hollered.

'I'm so excited!' Rachna said to Zaid.

Zaid squeezed her hand and smiled at her. They saw Tia walking towards them. 'Hey, guys! What's up?'

'We leave in ten minutes. I've been looking forward to Niagara and how!' The cold wind hit Rachna hard in the face and she shivered. 'Shit, it's freezing.'

Zaid drew her closer to keep her warm and she smiled up at him.

'I know! Winter is here,' Tia said in a sombre tone, referencing the *Game of Thrones*.

Rachna giggled. 'Oh, my God! That finale was ah-mazing! I can't wait for season seven,' she replied.

Zaid looked amused. Tia had been hanging out quite a bit with them and Rachna had really begun to hit it off with Tia. Zaid had begun joking about how they didn't need him around anymore because the girls chattered non-stop when they saw each other.

The International Students Organization volunteer continued calling out the names on her list and they yelled back and waved to her so she knew they were actually here. Then the volunteer called out Fiona's name, but there was no response. Zaid worriedly dialled her number. Rachna unthinkingly rolled her eyes and then glanced guiltily at Zaid to make sure he hadn't see her do that.

She knew Fiona was just his friend, but she hated that she was such a damsel in distress. Fiona called Zaid all the time to talk and she needed to meet with him constantly to share her life's woes. And Zaid would just drop whatever he was doing to go help her out. She knew Zaid was a loyal friend and someone who went out of his way to help others. Case in point: the night he stayed up with her to finish her assignment. But she kind of wished he would reserve his kindness for her. After all, his taking the time out to help her with her assignment that night was the turning point for her. That was when she really fell for him. That night, he made her feel special. But when she saw him going out of his way for Fiona, she started feeling that Zaid didn't differentiate between his friends and her. He was just that nice to everyone he knew. And that thought bummed her out.

She realized she had been staring into space so she snapped back to reality. She glanced at Tia who gave her a reassuring smile. Hmm. Did she sense Rachna's resentment of Fiona? Anyway, what was the deal with Fiona? Where was she? She looked up at Zaid; he was deep in conversation with her on his phone.

'Just come, Fi. It's going to be a lot of fun. I promise ... you don't have to make conversation with anyone. I'm there. And Rach and Tia ... you know them ... it's all good. You have five minutes to drag your ass down here, missy. If you're not here, I'm coming to get you myself ... do you want me to miss out on seeing Niagara because of you?' he asked.

He listened for a few seconds before he smiled and said, 'Great. Hurry up.'

Then he ran to the volunteer and proceeded to persuade her to wait until Fiona arrived.

Ten minutes later, panting, Fiona ran towards them. 'Hey' she smiled at all of them.

Zaid hugged her. 'Finally! Come on, let's go.'

Fiona and Tia walked ahead. Zaid took Rach's hand in his and they walked towards the bus. He continued to hold her hand as they boarded the bus and for the entire hour-and-a-half drive to Niagara Falls.

Rach closed her eyes and rested her head on his shoulder. She reminded herself that Zaid made her really happy. She wasn't going to let anyone or anything come between them. Not Fiona and definitely not her own insecurities and possessiveness.

The volunteer addressed the group over the amplifier system of the big bus: 'And we're here. Guys, stick together. We've got to get the tickets for the Maid of the

Mist. We'll see that together and then you guys can split up and do whatever you want.'

The Maid of the Mist was the boat tour of Niagara Falls. Zaid had read about it when he had googled Canada back when he was in South Africa. He was really looking forward to it.

All forty of the students on the trip queued up and they were given a raincoat each to wear over their clothes. When the boat began to move, Zaid was spellbound. The sheer magnificence of the waterfalls was astounding. At one point, all they could see around them was the water cascading from the falls. As if that wasn't stunning enough, they were greeted by the sight of two rainbows. Zaid had never seen anything so beautiful before. It was super romantic. He squeezed Rach's hand and in return she flashed him her biggest smile. Zaid was just so happy to be there with Rach. They took lots of pictures; he posed with Rach for all the pictures she wanted. And anyone who knew Zaid knew how much he hated being photographed. Even Fiona smiled a genuine smile upon seeing the falls. After the hellish weeks she had been through, she truly needed a break. Zaid had been very concerned about her while she battled through her depression. He had been trying to include her in as many of their outings as he could; and while she had somehow wriggled out of coming out with them eighty per cent of the time, Zaid managed to get her out of her room a few times at least. However, when she refused to come to Niagara, he would have none of it. It was a once in a lifetime experience. And, as he could vouch for that from personal experience, travel and new experiences are proven cures for unhappiness. He was glad he had bulldozed her into coming along.

'And now you guys can wander off. Just get back to this sign right here at five this evening, okay?' the volunteer said, indicating the gigantic 'Welcome to Niagara Falls' billboard.

They had four-and-a-half hours to do whatever they wanted. Although Rachna and Zaid could have splintered off from Fiona and Tia, Zaid was aware that Fiona wouldn't feel comfortable if she was left alone to make small talk with Tia. She just wasn't up for that yet. In a group, she would have the option to stay quiet. So he suggested the four of them spend the day together. That was when Rach got pissed off. Thankfully, she didn't make a public spectacle. She waited until they were about to enter a restaurant, to confront Zaid. Fi and Tia had already entered the restaurant to get a table.

'What the fuck, baby?' Rach attacked Zaid.

He was a little taken aback by the aggression.

'What?' he replied.

'You know what! We could have spent the day alone. Just the two of us. Why did you have to include Fiona and Tia in our plan?'

'Baby, Fiona is going through a really rough patch. I've told you she's having a hard time right now. She needs me. She needs us. I couldn't just abandon her. Especially after I was the one who persuaded her to come today. She has been so out of it, she really needed this today.'

'She needs this, she needs you, she's upset, she needs

to talk. What the fuck, man? What about me? Your girlfriend is the one who's allowed to be emotionally vulnerable and need you; not your friend! She's a grown up and can sort out her life on her own. It's good to be there for your friends but you need to be there for your girlfriend too! And you need to know where to draw the line with your friends. I'm not a possessive girlfriend. I'm not this psycho, insecure girl who can't deal with you having female friends. But we've only just started dating. We need to spend time together. Just the two of us. And she's always, always around. And if she's not physically present then she's calling you. Doesn't she have someone else she can talk to? I mean, she just met you two months ago! How did she manage before she met you?'

Where was all this coming from? He had been spending all his free time with Rach. Yes, he had included Fi in a few of their plans, but just because they were dating each other, it didn't mean that they wouldn't spend time with their friends too. He took a deep breath. He didn't want to create a scene and Fiona and Tia would start wondering why they weren't going in. 'Let's talk about this once we get back to campus. They must have gotten a table. Why don't we go join them and be normal? I'm pressing pause on this fight ... or disagreement rather,' he said calmly.

'Whatever. You know I'm right. You clearly care more about Fiona than you do about me. But I refuse to be taken for granted. I deserve someone who wants to spend time with me. I shouldn't have to beg for privacy. My boyfriend should *want* to have one-on-one time with me.' She stormed off into the restaurant.

Rach was distant for the rest of the day, speaking only with Tia during lunch. After lunch the group walked on the Street of Fun. The colourful street was lined with various restaurants and attractions like the Great Canadian Midway entertainment complex. They made a pit stop at the entertainment complex where Rach and Tia proceeded to play games like air hockey and foosball. Rach clearly wanted to keep her distance so Zaid entertained himself with the bike and car racing games. Fiona sat on a bench nearby. Zaid eventually convinced her to play some arcade games with him. Zaid felt Rach's eyes on him throughout the afternoon but when he would glance her way, she would look away.

When they were done with the arcade, they continued to walk on the street. Rach and Tia took pictures of each other wearing crazy hats and wigs at a shop and posed at the candy store and outside the Movieland Wax Museum of the Stars. Rach walked ahead with Tia on purpose leaving Zaid to walk with Fiona. Even Fiona who was lost in her thoughts the entire day, sensed that something was wrong.

'Everything okay?' she asked Zaid, as he walked alongside her.

'Uh, I guess. Just a small disagreement.'

'Don't worry, it will be okay. I really like Rach. She's really cool,' Fiona said.

If only she knew how Rach felt about her, Fiona would have sung a whole different tune.

Zaid didn't intend on telling her so he just smiled at Fiona and nodded.

On the ride back home, Rach fell asleep and rested her head on the window instead of Zaid's shoulder.

Zaid just sighed and stared into space for the rest of the bus ride.

When they got off the bus on campus, Zaid considered reasoning with Rach. But before he could say anything she began walking off in the opposite direction. She was clearly not interested in being reasonable.

'Bye,' Zaid muttered and started walking to his residence building.

Rach didn't reply. Zaid wondered where she was going; her building was in the same direction as his. She would probably wait for him to reach his flat and then walk to hers. He would have laughed at them if he were an objective observer. But when you're in a relationship and in the midst of a fight, somehow things don't seem that funny.

He sighed. He didn't know how they got here. The trip to Niagara that had started out on a promising note, suddenly fell completely apart.

An hour later, he was lying in bed watching a movie. He hadn't spent an evening alone in a long time. He had forgotten how lonely living alone could get.

His mind drifted back to Rach. The only reason she was so unsympathetic towards Fiona was because she didn't know what Fiona had to deal with in the last few weeks. Rach was a compassionate person. If she knew about Fiona's abortion, she was bound to understand why Zaid had been so attentive to Fiona. But he had promised Fi that he would guard her secret. She didn't want her life to become a piece of juicy gossip shared on campus. And Zaid respected that. Nevertheless, Rach's being in the dark about Fi's pregnancy was impeding his romantic relationship. He wondered whether he should ask Fi and tell Rach about it.

But Fi seemed to be slowly recovering and getting back to being her old self. She was quiet in Niagara that day but there were times during the trip when she had allowed herself to let her hair down and truly enjoy herself. It would be unfair to remind her of everything when she needed so badly to forget. Perhaps he was just making too much of it. He would just give Rach a day to calm down and then sort everything out with her tomorrow.

Everything was going to be fine, he was sure of it.

'So I'll see you in the quad at six?' Tia asked Rach over the phone while checking herself out in the mirror. God, she had really gained the dreaded Freshman 15. But when she had literally been surviving on pizza, burgers and all the other junk food uni had to offer, what else did she think would happen?

'I don't know. I'm not even sure I want to go to this thing,' Rach said. She sounded completely out of it. Tia couldn't see her face but could tell something was wrong from the tone of her voice.

'What? No way, Rach! You're coming!' Tia shrieked.

Rach groaned. 'Okay fine. But I didn't have time to go outfit shopping. I just have that dumb long black wig that we brought back from Niagara.'

'Okay, that's fine. We can work with that. Um. Oh, I

know! How about Morticia from the *Addams Family*? Didn't you tell me how much you loved the *Addams Family* growing up?'

'Wow, you really listen when I talk, Ti! I wish you were my boyfriend! Well, not in *that* way. Just that you're such a good listener. You know what I mean,' she said.

Tia laughed. 'Yes, yes, I know what you mean. I don't think you're in love with me, don't worry. Anyway, so? What do you say? Is Morticia a winner? You can wear your black dress, leggings and boots. And then just apply lots of foundation. Crimson lipstick. And dark eye make-up of course. And voila! You're done!'

'Sure. It doesn't require much work so it suits me just fine. Anyway, how has your look turned out?'

'Good, I think! Just that my ass looks big, but then that has nothing to do with the dress.'

'No, dude! I've told you so many times, your ass is fine. It's not big. At all. Relax,' Rach said.

It was a blatant lie but Tia appreciated Rach's attempt at trying to make her feel better. 'Anyhoo, I've got class now. I'll see you at six. Bye.'

Tia hung up and got out of her costume. She was super late for class but she felt like talking to Armaan. Plus, he would appreciate the costume. If only he were here, she had a feeling he would really enjoy stripping her out of her ensemble. She'd asked Armaan for some time to figure out her feelings for him but turned out she didn't really need that much time after all. She hadn't stopped thinking about him ever since he confessed to liking her. But God, long-distance relationships were so hard. And man, oh man, was she horny right now. Hmmm. She wondered if she had time to ... yeah ... no ... bad idea. She snapped back to reality and decided to just Facetime with Armaan when she was completely ready in the evening. And she reminded herself that January was just two months away.

Tia couldn't help smiling on her walk to the University Centre. There was a sea of costumes all around her. There were the usual suspects – pirates, cops, nurses and vampires. And then there were the really innovative ones – she just espied a guy dressed as Ron Swanson from *Parks and Recreation* with a girl dressed as a burger. Then there was a girl wearing a 'Netflix' T-shirt and a guy wearing a 'Chill' T-shirt holding an ice tray for good measure. She suddenly noticed the back of a girl with long black hair, sporting a black, knee-length dress with black boots. She totally looked the part. 'Good job, girlfriend,' she shouted out.

Rach turned around. Her eyes widened when she saw Tia.

'Woah! Look at you! Good job, yourself. This is the perfect costume to go with your red hair. Love it! Melisandre is hot!' Rach exclaimed as Tia twirled in her red maxi dress. Tia had decided to honour her obsession with *Game of Thrones* through her costume.

'Why thank you, bae! This is why I love you. You know exactly how to make a girl's day.'

'Where did you get the choker from?' Rach asked.

'Oh, I borrowed it from Leigh.'

'Ah. Didn't Leigh want to come today?'

'She has a big paper tomorrow. Plus, she's not that excited about trick-or-treating; having done it only for the first thirteen years of her life.'

Rach nodded. 'I trick-or-treated until I was thirteen too. I used to love Halloween. God, I miss being a kid.'

'Well, in India, we've been going to Halloween parties for the last two years so I've done the costume part before. But I love that I get to go trick-or-treating. Even if I'm nineteen years too late.'

The university had organized a trick-or-treating experience with a difference. Those who signed up were supposed to collect canned goods from houses in Guelph and donate them to the needy. The idea was to have fun while supporting a great cause.

Rachna and Tia had covered ten houses in the last fifteen minutes and everyone had been really generous with their donations. Most of the residents knew about the canned food collection drive and had kept their donations ready. The owner of the second house offered the girls candy as soon as he opened the door but Rach explained to him that they were looking for canned food and not candy. The same thing happened with house number three. Just before they walked to house number four, Tia felt like she had to say something.

'Rach, you don't have to ask for the donation immediately! Let them give us some candy first and then we can collect the donation? It's my first, and probably only, trick-or-treating experience. I need some treats, yo!' Tia said through chattering teeth.

Rachna laughed, but agreed.

It was freezing and Tia regretted not wearing her jacket over her dress. She thought the coat would ruin the effect of her costume but clearly it was a bad decision. She shivered and linked arms with Rachna as they walked to the next house on their list.

'So, is everything okay between Zaid and you?' Tia got right to it.

'What? Uh? Why?'

'Nothing, it's just that you started ignoring him at Niagara last week. And you guys are clearly still fighting because you've not been your cheery self. So, what's up?'

Rachna hesitated for a few seconds before finally saying, 'Yeah, Zaid and I aren't talking. We fought last week about Fiona. I hate how she's so needy when it comes to Zaid. I mean, first she pulled the whole "I'm not coming to Niagara" thing and Zaid had to call and cajole her into coming. She was literally there five minutes after she spoke with Zaid, so she clearly wanted to come all along. So why the whole "not coming" act? And I don't like how Zaid has to ensure that Fiona is okay all the time. Isn't the entire "damsel-in-distress" act so 1920? It's just so bloody annoying. I can't stand her.'

Tia let Rach vent because she knew that sometimes all you really needed was someone to hear you out. When Rach finished her rant she looked at Tia expectantly. Tia decided to weigh her words. She thought Rach was overreacting; she was just being possessive of her boyfriend. Fiona didn't come across as the needy, attention-deprived person Rach thought she was. And Zaid was a loyal, sweet guy. You could tell he really liked

Rach. She was just creating problems for herself. But Tia knew she needed to address the matter cautiously so she said, 'I can see why as a girlfriend Fiona's dependency on Zaid bugs you. I'm in a long-distance relationship so I don't know what it's like to see your boyfriend being attentive towards another woman. But based on what I know about Zaid, he genuinely is a sweet, nice guy. Don't be too hard on him. And don't let a nice guy go for no real reason. There aren't too many of them around.'

They reached a house by then so Rach didn't get to respond immediately. They collected their tinned food and candy (wow, this particular house had been really generous!) and continued walking.

'I know you're right, but I also feel like I should be the number one priority in my boyfriend's life. And I know he's not cheating on me – I trust him completely. But Fiona is coming in the way of our relationship. She just really pisses me off.' Rach took a deep breath.

Tia nodded. 'Well, don't worry, Rach. Everything will work out. I really believe that when relationships are meant to work, they do. So don't get stressed out.' Tia squeezed Rach's hand.

Rach gave Tia a quick hug. She looked at her watch. 'Oh, wow, it's already ten to eight. We have time to do just one more house. Come on, girlfriend, let's go score more candy!'

An hour later, they were back at uni and in Tia's room. Rach and Tia were splitting the candy they had collected. 'This stash is amazing! Go team,' Rach said, high-fiving Tia.

'Yeah, but I think we should go work off the ten Toblerone bars we've just eaten, Rach.' Tia said, eyeing her protruding stomach in the mirror on her cupboard. 'You ready to go to the Mountain Hall party?'

Rach was busy staring at her phone. 'What?' she asked distractedly.

'Should we head to Mountain?'

'Yeah, I guess.'

They wrapped their woollen coats closer to their bodies as they walked to the building. There was no doubt now that winter was officially here. When they reached the building, they ran up the stairs and heaved a sigh of relief as soon as they were ensconced in the warmth of the hallway.

'Chug! Chug! Chug!' There were feverish chants as a guy and girl were having a beer-drinking contest in the centre of the room.

The guy gave up and the girl was declared the winner of the game.

She wiped her mouth and burped loudly and everyone cheered for her. Because she was a hot girl, of course. If she wasn't pretty and skinny and had pulled a feat like that, no one would care as much, Tia thought ruefully. But that was a debate for another day.

'Beer?' she asked Rach.

'Yes please,' Rach said as they headed towards the table with the drinks.

And that's when it happened. Rach spotted them first. Tia looked at her ashen face and then followed her gaze.

Standing by the drinks table were Zaid and Fiona. He handed her a drink, they clinked their red plastic beer mugs.

He whispered something in her ear and she smiled at him.

Then he looked in their direction. His expression changed too. He placed his drink on the table and walked towards Rach and Tia. But Rach was done. She turned around and literally ran out of the party.

'Rach! Wait!' both Zaid and Tia called out in unison. But she was having none of it.

Tia considered following her, but she knew Rach needed some time to be alone. Zaid looked at Tia helplessly. Tia gave him a small reassuring smile.

NOVEMBER

Rachna lay in bed polishing off her Halloween candy stash with a vengeance. Her phone beeped and she didn't jump at it as she usually did. Whoever it was and whatever they had to say, she simply didn't care. Everyone sucked. All she needed was her candy, which would never let her down; it tasted as good as its packaging promised. With people, however, you could never tell. Take Zaid for instance. He came across as a sweet, sensitive, nice guy (well, after he was done with his bitchy stuck-up phase at the beginning of uni), but what did he turn out to be? Just a typical guy. He couldn't handle all the attention he was getting from ... uh ... she didn't even want to take her name. And ultimately, her neediness won. She acted like she couldn't do without him and so he felt needed and wanted. And Rachna? Well, with her whole I'm-an-independent-strong-woman-who-doesn't-need-you stance, it appears she had lost the guy.

She felt a tear threaten to spill any moment now. She was in the safety of her room, even so she didn't want to cry. Why should she cry for him when he was out at parties with she-who-shall-not-be-named, having the time of his life?

There was a knock at her door and she jumped. It was probably her roommate, Janice. Perhaps if she pretended she wasn't here, Janice would go away. But the knocking persisted. When she couldn't take it anymore, she shouted, 'Who is it? I'm a little busy right now.'

There was no reply, but the knocking continued. Argh! Rachna was going to kill her.

She clambered out of bed, scattering candy wrappers like confetti all over the room.

'What! What do you want?' she yelled, flinging open the door.

It was not Janice. It was she-who-shall-not-be-named. What the hell was she doing here? She wore an apologetic look. Rachna's initial surprise at seeing her was replaced by fury. She glared at her.

'Uh, hi Rach. I know you hate me right now. But I need to talk to you,' Fiona said.

Rachna was torn between not wanting to hear her voice and wanting to know what she had to say.

'Come in,' she finally said in a gruff voice.

Fiona seemed a little taken aback by the mess in Rachna's room. So, she was neater than Rachna too? This was just great. She sat on the chair at the desk across from Rachna who perched on the edge of her bed.

'Rachna, I need to talk to you. I ... I ... uh, I guess I've come between Zaid and you. You have to believe me when I say that that was never my intention. Zaid is just a friend. No wait, that's a lie.'

Rachna's heartbeat quickened. Oh gosh. So here it was. Rachna's suspicions confirmed; Fiona was going to admit to liking Zaid.

'Zaid has become my best friend. He stood by me when I was all alone and had no one else to count on. And what's more, he has guarded my secret, at the cost of his own relationship. I don't know too many people who would have done that,' she continued.

Fiona took a deep breath. 'I haven't told anyone about this. Other than Zaid, no one else knows about this. I … um … I got pregnant. It was Arjun.'

Rachna's eyes widened. Woah. This she had not seen coming.

'I really liked Arjun. And I obviously freaked out when I discovered that I was pregnant. I wish that were the end of the story. But there's more. When I went to tell Arjun about it, I caught him in bed. And that too with my "best friend", Natalie. I told Zaid about it. And he has been wonderful. He took me to the hospital for my abortion. And he included me in your plans so that I could get out more. He didn't want me to sink into depression. Which honestly, was a real likelihood. But, of course, you guys are in a new relationship and you need your space. And I've been so caught up in my own misery, that I never realized the impact I had on your relationship.'

'Oh, fuck. I mean … uh … I had no idea. I'm … I'm sorry you had to go through all of this Fiona,' Rachna said. Fiona looked so vulnerable. Rachna felt like reaching out and giving her a hug. No wonder Zaid felt like protecting her too.

Fiona shrugged. 'Ah. Shit happens, right? I won't say I'm completely over my crap. But I'm definitely doing better. And I only have Zaid to thank for this. I won't stop saying it – he has been an amazing friend. It was like God sent someone when I needed help the most. I'm still overwhelmed by how wonderful he has been. He really didn't have to do any of it, but he did. So, yeah, that's my story.'

Everything made sense. It explained why Zaid was so pissed off with Arjun at the cultural show after-party and why Fiona left early. It also explained Fiona's reluctance to come on the Niagara trip. And also why Zaid went out of his way to ensure that she did.

'Wow. Not in a good way of course. I mean, this is a lot to take in. I feel like a really petty bitch now, actually. You were going through something so huge. In comparison, I had ... have ... no problems. And I gave Zaid such a hard time.' She shook her head in remorse.

Fiona reached out for Rachna's hand. 'It's okay. You had no idea. I would have probably reacted in the same way if I were you. You obviously really like Zaid. And he is definitely smitten by you. So you must make it okay with him.'

Rachna rose from the bed, went over to Fiona and gave her a tight hug. Fiona was a little stiff at first, but then after a moment, she hugged Rach back.

'Thank you. And sorry. I misunderstood you and how. You're really strong. I don't think I would have handled the whole situation so well if I were you,' Rach said to her.

'Ah, well, I had no option but to be strong I guess.'

Fiona left and Rachna replayed the last few weeks in her head, armed with her new knowledge.

Zaid had been staring at the same page for the last hour. He just couldn't concentrate. He had had a lot on his mind in the last week, obviously. And because he didn't know what to say to Rach, he had conveniently taken the coward's route by not saying anything to her. When she saw Fiona and him talking at the party yesterday, she must have thought they were more than friends. It was like God, or the universe, or something cosmic, didn't want them to be together. Why else would there be so many obstacles to something which should be effortless? The timing had all been disastrously off. Rach and he were happy and everything had been perfect. And then Fiona got pregnant. Zaid didn't for one minute regret supporting Fiona and being there for her when she needed him; but he couldn't blame Rach for feeling upset.

He couldn't forget the look in her eyes when she saw Fiona and him at the party yesterday. She hadn't looked angry; she looked incredibly sad and heartbroken. He had never wanted to see that pain in Rach's eyes. Ever. He couldn't believe how deeply he had hurt the person he loved. She didn't deserve this. He had no right to do this to her.

Suddenly he knew what he needed to do. He had to tell Fiona that Rach and his relationship was suffering due to a misunderstanding and ask Fiona's permission to share her secret with Rach. And then he would have to come clean with Rach. He couldn't give up on Rach and what they had just like that. He had wasted too much time already; he needed to make things right.

He rose from his desk, threw his jacket on and walked out of his room purposefully only to find Rachna standing in the lounge of his apartment.

She smiled in response to his bewildered expression. She held a huge bowl of popcorn in her hands. She gestured to her laptop placed on the coffee table.

'Would you like to watch the *Blind Side* with me?' she asked.

'What? Huh?' was all Zaid managed to say.

'Why don't you sit down?'

She sat on the couch next to Zaid. She took his hand in hers and said, 'Fiona came to see me this morning. She told me everything. About the pregnancy, about Arjun being a cheating jerk and about how wonderful you've been to her through it all. I feel terrible. I can't believe how badly I overreacted. I just had no idea. I guess you never really know what battles people are fighting. I wish I had known what Fiona was going through; I would never have acted the way I did. And I wish you had told me, but you did an honourable thing by safeguarding her secret. I understand why you couldn't tell me.'

He couldn't believe this was really happening. So there is a God! He was so taken aback that he was speechless for a few moments.

'What? Are you still upset with me? I'm sorry for the way I behaved, but I didn't know ...'

He reached out, cupped her face and kissed her gently. She couldn't believe the effect he had on her every time their lips met. She didn't want the kiss to end but she needed to know everything was okay between them.

'So, we're good then?' she asked, breathlessly.

'Yes! Isn't that obvious? I ... I'm so happy you're here, Rach. You have no idea how happy I am to see you. I've missed you so much. And I was actually on my way to see you just now. I wanted to make things right between us. You're the best thing that has happened to me in a long time. And I'm not going to let go,' he said.

It was her turn to kiss him. She put her hands around the back of his head and drew his lips towards hers. 'Same here. So should we go watch the movie in your room?'

'Uh ... yes! Is that even a question? Great choice of movie by the way.'

'I figured since I ruined your experience watching the movie once, I owed you a movie-watching session without interruptions,' she responded, eyes twinkling.

'Oh, I think there will be interruptions.' He winked at her.

She laughed that gorgeous laugh of hers and Zaid couldn't help but think how lucky he was to have found her.

'Can you pass the butter chicken, Z?' Fiona asked.

Zaid passed the dish to her across the table. They were seated around a wooden table in the centre of the Diana Downtown restaurant – his favourite Indian restaurant in Guelph. Zaid and Rachna had stumbled across it last week and had raved about the food to all their friends. The décor was minimalistic and the food was to die for.

'Sorry I'm late, guys. Stupid finance lecture just wouldn't let up!' Tia bustled into the restaurant.

'It's okay. Breathe, Tia. Come, sit.' Rachna gestured to the empty chair on her left.

Tia flopped into the chair. She inhaled the aroma of Indian spices and said, 'Ooh, yum! I'm starving,' as she scooped the samosas, gravies and naans laid out on the table into her plate.

'Gosh, I've missed Indian food and how,' Fiona said through a mouthful of food.

'You can say that again. I've been craving aloo parathas like crazy this week. Man, I miss my mum,' Rach added.

'Me too,' Zaid, Fiona and Tia said in unison. Everyone stared into space, clearly reminiscing about home.

'Okay, come on, guys. Cheer up. Hey, didn't get a chance to wish you. Happy Diwali, Tia!' Zaid said. 'I know you're all missing home. You can't help but feel lonely when you're away from all the celebrations. I mean, I can only imagine how I'd feel if I were missing Eid with my mum and cousins. Festivals are all about family. But I think what's most important is to spend festivals with the people you love.' Zaid looked at Rach when he said the last bit and she smiled warmly at him.

'Friends can become your family. And sitting a thousand miles from home, I can safely say that you guys have all become my family for sure. I know we have each other's backs and that's something I'm really grateful for. So Happy Diwali, guys! Cheers!' Zaid raised his drink and clinked it with Rach, Fiona and Tia.

'Happy Diwali,' the girls chorused.

'Hey, is that alcohol you're drinking?' Tia asked, as she sipped her water. 'I never did back home because we would be doing Laxmi pooja right about now.'

'Well my mum doesn't follow the whole not-drinking thing during Diwali. And being half-Christian half-Hindu, I've never known what the protocol is either. But the last thing I need right now is to piss off Laxmi Mata, so I think I'm sticking to Sprite. God knows I can do without any more bad luck,' Fi replied.

Tia looked a little baffled by Fiona's statement. She was the only one in the group who didn't know about Fiona's misadventure. Rach noticed Tia's expression and quickly changed the topic.

'Okay, so we won't drink tonight. But we can stuff our faces for sure! I know I'm saving some space for gulab jamuns.'

Rach whispered to Fiona, 'Everything's going to be fine, Fi-fi. Trust me.'

Zaid squeezed Rach's hand. He was delighted that everyone was finally getting along. Things had been great with Rach. In fact, tonight might actually be the night that he would get lucky. Wait, unless she thought God might get upset if they did it on Diwali! Okay, maybe not tonight ... but soon. Truth be told, he was happy just spending time with her. He couldn't believe he had found happiness with someone else. After Devi, he thought his heart would never mend. And even if he had a flicker of hope that he would find love again, he thought it would happen a few years down the line. He certainly didn't expect it to happen so soon. He knew he shouldn't use the word 'love'. Rach and he had decided to steer clear of the 'L' word. Especially because he was going back to Durban at the end of this semester. Suddenly the thought of going back depressed him no end. It wasn't just about leaving Rach. It was everything. As lost as he had felt when he first arrived, the University of Guelph had now become his home. He couldn't believe it had happened in a span of just ten weeks, but it had.

'I'll miss you. I lo ... I mean ... I "live" you,' Rach smiled as she kissed Zaid on the cheek. They had decided not to complicate things by saying 'I love you' to each other. So they had coined a term together; 'live', which was more than 'like' and a lot like 'love'.

She was lying in bed with Zaid. He had his arms wrapped tightly around her and he refused to let her go.

'No. You can't go,' he protested.

'Come on, baby. You know I have to. I've missed two econ lectures this week. I'll fail at this rate.'

'No you won't. You're super smart. It's one of the reasons I lo ... I mean "live" you.'

'Okay now, I've really got to go. See you at five.'

She extricated herself from his embrace and rushed off.

Zaid sighed. He should probably get out of bed too. His first class was in an hour. Hmmm. A quick fifteen-minute nap wouldn't hurt. He shut his eyes and pulled the blanket closer around him.

He was sound asleep when he heard the incessant knocking on his room door. Rach probably forgot her phone or something. He got out of bed and opened the door.

'Did you forget something, ba—?' He stopped short when he saw who it was. Standing in the doorway was Arjun.

Although Zaid saw him almost every day at class, Zaid had ceased to acknowledge him. Several times, Arjun had tried approaching him post their classes, but Zaid would just walk away. However now, slamming the door in his face seemed rude. He might as well hear the guy out.

'Yes?'

'Hey, man. Can I come in?'

Zaid hesitated for a few seconds and then stood back to let him in. Arjun flopped on the couch in the lounge with the ease of familiarity. Zaid thought back to all the times that Arjun had sat on that very couch when they had shared a laugh and beers.

'So uh … I really wanted to talk to you. The term is ending soon and I don't know for how long you're in Canada, but I didn't want to leave things on a bad note. I … I … uh … recently had a reality check. My dad—' he started and stopped, as his eyes filled with tears. Zaid stared in disbelief. Arjun Cool-Guy Cheistwer was crying? He didn't even know the guy had emotions. He usually laughed his way through the gravest of situations.

'My dad had a heart attack two weeks ago.'

'Oh shit, I'm sorry. Is he okay?'

'Yeah, luckily it was a mild attack. But waiting outside his hospital room has been one of the hardest things I've ever had to do. It was also the loneliest I've ever felt. My mum was in Dubai on a work trip when it happened, so it took her two days to get there. My brother has only just moved to Singapore, so we told him to not rush back. When the doctor assured us that Dad would be fine, we asked Aryan not to come at all. Anyway, the point is, I desperately wanted to talk to someone; I needed a shoulder to cry on. And I realized I had no one. I have so many "friends" I can party with. Too many, in fact, but very few with whom I can actually have a meaningful conversation. And all the things you told me at the culture show came rushing back to me.'

Zaid thought back to the culture show after-party. He was livid when he had seen Arjun drinking and having a great time at the do a mere five days after Fiona had aborted their child. She was depressed and broken and he was oblivious to what he had done.

'I haven't met a more selfish, self-obsessed, inconsiderate douche in my entire life, Arjun. You might be a really good-looking guy and all the ladies love you and whatever, but you're a terrible person. You broke my friend's heart and scarred her for life. And for that I'm never going to forgive you.'

At the time, Arjun had said, 'Woah, woah! Chill out, Zaid. Please ask Fiona; had I ever told her that we were exclusive? Did I ever refer to her as "my girlfriend"? Did I tell her I like her? She's an adult. She knew exactly what she was getting into. We were just two people attracted to each other and having sex. I can't help it if she built a relationship in her head. That was all her. *I* never committed to anything.'

'You got her pregnant, you asshole! And when she came to break the news to you, she found you in bed with her best friend! Don't you have a frikkin' conscience? D'you know how upset Fiona was? D'you know how much she cried at the clinic before going in for the surgery? No, of course you don't. Because you're a selfish asshole.'

'She got pre … pregnant? But how? We used protection every time. Except maybe that one time …' he trailed off as he realized when it had happened.

'Yeah, that one time that you were too fuckin' lazy or drunk to find a condom, ended up screwing up Fiona's life. I've seen her deal with emotions a nineteen-year-old should never have to deal with. She feels guilty about having ended a life, she was heartbroken that she fell for a douche like you, she was lonely because she couldn't count on her family for support during her ordeal, she feels like she has broken her parents' trust. In short, she is messed up. She has had the toughest week of her life. And you – you've been partying and I'm assuming fucking around like nothing's happened. So, forgive me if I'm not "chill" about this. But honestly, I'd much rather be uptight than be as chilled out as you. Because, in your case, "being chilled out" translates into being insensitive and self-centred. And I would never want to be you.'

Zaid had coldly stalked back into the hall after that.

'I was shocked by everything you said to me that day. I knew I should talk to Fiona but I couldn't bring myself to face her. And then, as I usually do, I convinced myself that everything that had happened was unfortunate, but wasn't really my fault. None of it was intentional. I missed hanging out with Fiona and you, but I still had tons of other people to party with. Every time I saw you in class,

I wanted to talk to you, but when you made it clear that you weren't interested in talking to me, I just gave up.'

He continued, 'Anyway, it was only when I was in that scary hospital waiting room, unsure whether my father would make it or not, that I got it. I got how scared Fiona must have felt going in for surgery. How alone she must have felt. And I got how selfish I've been. I've never taken anything seriously. I've been so focused on having fun, that I forgot that life isn't all fun and games all the time. I've always run away from difficult situations. But I think facing things head on is part of growing up. So I went to Fiona's apartment today, before coming to yours.'

This warranted a response. 'What did she say?'

'She cried. She didn't really say much. She said the wounds are too fresh for her to forgive me. But she said she's in a much better place now than she was a month ago. And she said that for her the one good thing that came out of meeting me, was meeting you. Of course, if she hadn't met me, she wouldn't be in a situation where she needed your support to begin with. Anyway, I just want you to know that I'm glad I met you too. We had some really fun times, Zaid. And you've taught me what it means to be a good guy. When I grow up, I want to be you.' Arjun grinned.

Zaid couldn't help but grin at that too. The guy knew how to win people over, that was for sure. 'I'm glad you finally get it. I'm sorry your dad had to get sick for you to get what I was talking about. I was pretty harsh at the culture show party. I was really pissed off at you then.'

'I deserved it.' Arjun nodded.

'We have had great times. I had completely isolated myself when I got here. I got back to being my true self, thanks to you. I'm sorry about how things worked out eventually. For what it's worth, I am glad I met you, Arjun. Despite everything. You're right, you know. I'm going back to Durban in two weeks' time and I don't know when I'll get to meet everyone again. The last thing I want is to leave on a bad note. I just want to take back good memories and leave good memories too.'

Arjun held out his hand for a handshake, but Zaid hugged him instead.

'Take care, man. Stay in touch,' Zaid said.

DECEMBER

FIONA

I tap my feet impatiently as the serpentine immigration queue at the Delhi airport moves at a snail's pace. What does it mean when the queue for foreigners is shorter than the one for Indian passport holders? Jeez! Are we being punished for being Indian in India?

Forty minutes later, and I'm finally moving towards the exit at the airport. Mum and Dad are waiting for me in the parking lot. I walk as fast as I can. After waiting another twenty minutes for the elevator to level P4 (every time the elevator doors open, there are already ten thousand people inside the elevator), I finally manage to get to the parking lot. I push my luggage trolley, scanning the parking lot for my parents. That's when I spot Kevin carrying a bunch of balloons standing next to a grey Honda Mobilio. I rush towards him. He spots me too and his face breaks into a huge smile.

'Hey, bum! I missed you, man.' I draw him into a hug.

'Ugh! Get off me!' he says, glancing around self-consciously. Like any of his lame friends would be here.

'Shut up and stop acting cool. No one is looking at you and no one cares, okay?' I mock yell at him. Of course, I was worse when I was his age. Ah! To be fifteen again!

My parents step out of the car and I hug them. 'I missed you so much, Mom' I say, hugging her tight.

'And what about me?' Dad asks.

'Of course, I missed you too, Dad. I'm so happy to be back.'

'Missed you, kiddo. And do you like the new car?'

'Oh yeah, it's pretty impressive. No wonder I couldn't spot you earlier. I forgot I wasn't looking for the old car. Good job on the upgrade, Dad.' Dad had bought a new car around the same time that I had had the ... uh ... abortion. I don't like saying the word 'abortion' but well, it is what it is. Mum had sent me a picture of the entire family posing in front of the car at the time. I had desperately wanted to be a part of that picture and somehow wake up to realize that I had never gotten pregnant and that it had all just been a bad dream.

'You're fine, aren't you, my baby?' Mom asked a little anxiously, perhaps my sadness had set off a blip on her maternal radar. 'I got so worried when you wouldn't reply to my messages. For almost three weeks, you barely spoke to us for five minutes before hanging up abruptly.' Mom was referring to that dark period when I just couldn't speak with my parents. I didn't know what to say to them. And I was terrified that I would break down and tell them the ugly truth.

'I'm fine, Mom. As I told you, that was a very hectic

time. I had way too many assignments and tests. I barely had time to eat; let alone chat.'

On the drive home, my parents continue to badger me with questions about uni and the friends I've made. Kevin, as materialistic and acquisitive as ever, only wants to know what I bought him. And I enquire about all the moments I missed. All the mundane things that I took for granted before moving, now seem extremely precious. The day my family bought the new car, the weekend trip they took in the car to Nainital, Kevin's birthday, Diwali, the time my aunt visited for a week, movies, dinner, Grandma's grumpiness, the maids' tantrums ... man, I missed my family.

To say it has been a challenging year would be an understatement. But as I inhale the cold December air, I find myself relaxing. I'm home with the people I love. And Christmas is ten days away. I may have veered completely off course this year, but what's important is that I'm back on track now.

I think back to when Arjun came to see me two weeks ago.

'Hi Fiona. This will only take a minute. I know you hate my guts and don't want to talk to me. But I owe you an apology. And while I don't expect you to forgive me, I do hope we can get some closure,' he said as soon as I had opened my door.

'What closure? We weren't in a relationship, remember? I just read too much into things. It was all "fun", right? It was the most "fun" I had ever had in my entire life. In fact, the "fun" didn't stop for me even after we stopped sleeping together. The party just continued,' I said, sarcastically.

'I deserve that. Ever since Zaid told me about ... uh ... the pregnancy ... I knew I had to face you. But, I didn't have the courage. And I didn't realize just how badly I had messed up either – until recently. I had a ... well ... I won't go into the details, but I had a personal crisis recently which served as a wake-up call and that kinda made me realize just how badly I had screwed up with you.'

'Don't cry. Don't cry. Don't show him you're weak,' I thought. But before I knew it, I could feel the hot tears spilling down my face.

He reached out to hug me, but I put my hand up to ward him off.

'I'm sorry, Fiona. I really, truly am. I'm sorry I ruined your first semester at college. No one should have to go through the kind of stress and pain you went through. I didn't mean to hurt you, but I was a selfish jerk. You're an amazing person. You deserve nothing but the best. And I'm sorry I ruined your friendship with Natalie.'

He stood around awkwardly for a few moments while I remained silent.

'I should go. Take care,' he said, before walking out of my apartment.

After he left, I shut the door and lay down for a while. At the time, I wasn't sure whether Arjun's apology had made me feel better or not. But now when I think back, I think it was good that that had happened. It was good to get closure; it was like the final painful cut in a surgery, after which I could only get better.

As for Natalie, she had continued to try to talk to

me every time we bumped into each other in the small space of our flat. After Arjun left my apartment that day, I thought about things from Natalie's perspective. She had screwed up with a friend and she had immediately apologized. Unlike Arjun, who hadn't had the guts to face me the entire time. And who self-admittedly didn't even realize the gravity of his actions until recently. So perhaps Natalie wasn't the evil, selfish bitch I had made her out to be. She was just a fun-loving person who chose to live in the moment. She was a tad self-centred, yes, but she wasn't necessarily a bad person. So I decided to forgive her. It was the only way for me to move on. But I also knew that we could never go back to what we were. Too much had happened for things to ever be normal between us again. So, on the last day of the semester, I went to her room. The door was ajar; she was packing her bag. She looked surprised when she saw me.

'Nat, I'm finally ready to talk to you. I appreciate you trying to make things okay between us. But, here's the thing; there's a lot of stuff that happened with Arjun that you don't know about. I don't want to talk about that, but I was justified in feeling heartbroken, upset and angry with both of you. I'm now ready to move on with my life, so I want to tell you that I forgive you. I don't hold a grudge against you anymore. But I really can't go back to being friends with you again. It was good while it lasted, but I'm moving on from this friendship. I'm going to try and live in another res or off-campus next semester, so seeing each other every day won't be an issue. Happy holidays, Nat. Bye,' I said and walked off.

I felt a weight lift off my shoulders that day. I was done holding on to my anger. I was finally free.

I spend the next two weeks catching up with old friends and family. We even go on a four-day holiday to Nainital. My parents planned it because I kept moaning about having missed the earlier family trip because I was in Canada. I laugh, sing and eat copious amounts of food during Christmas.

When it's time for me to board my flight back to Toronto, I almost feel like my old self. As I wave goodbye to my parents before heading to the check-in counter, I have a sense of déjà vu. I remember how excited I had been to start my new life in Canada as I walked to this very counter four months ago. Only then, I was naïve. And now, even though I'm optimistic about the future, I'm much wiser. I've definitely become a better judge of character. You know what they say: once screwed, twice wary.

RACHNA

'So, this poor guy, Aaron, had like never even kissed a girl. Total nerd,' Jo says.

'And all the girls on our dorm floor decided to give him the best (or was it the worst?) birthday surprise ever,' Amy continues.

'Picture this. He walked into his room and saw a stripper poised on his chair, just waiting for him. And then all of us burst into his room and yelled, "SURPRISE!" He got the shock of his life. And then, the stripper proceeded to give him a thorough lap dance and even kissed him. All this while, the rest of us cheered them on and recorded it on our phones. Poor Aaron. He was as red as a beet.' Jo giggles.

'You should have been there, Rach. We had the time of our lives,' Amy concludes.

I smile at Amy and Jo. 'Uni definitely sounds like a blast, guys. And as much as I would have enjoyed doing uni here with you guys, I'm happy I chose to go to Canada. I've had some adventures of my own. And met people I never would have met if I had been too scared to get out of my comfort zone.'

'Absolutely, Rach. Your pictures at Niagara were stunning. We should plan a trip to visit you in Canada next year,' Amy says.

'For sure. But, enough about all that.' Jo winks at me. 'Give us more details on the boyfriend. Hello! Did you guys ... you know ... hmmm .... hmmm?'

I can feel the blood rush to my cheeks. 'We did. The

first two or three times were painful. But then, it was sooo good. Although honestly, I enjoy the kissing and foreplay way more than the actual act, you know?'

'Oooh! Miss Virgin-No-More! This is huge! Look at you ... all grown up with a boyfriend!' Amy squeals.

'Well, it is a little unbelievable sometimes. At first I just met a bunch of idiots and I really despaired that I was destined to be single forever. And then, Zaid happened.'

'But you said he was an exchange student for just one semester, right? So, what now? How are you guys going to make this work?' Jo enquires.

My face falls as the reality of my situation hits me again. I fill Amy and Jo in on how Zaid has spoken to his university back in Durban. He might be able to do one more semester as an exchange student. Winter semester begins in three weeks and they should know if his application for another semester has been accepted or not in a week's time. Luckily his student visa is valid for one year anyway, so at least he doesn't have to apply for another visa. I've been praying he gets to do one more semester but I'm also preparing myself for the worst-case scenario. He might not come back to Guelph next semester and I'm going to have to be okay with that. We're crazy about each other and we're still going to make our relationship work; I don't care what the sceptics say about long-distance relationships.

Still, it's hard to imagine campus without him. My mind wanders back to the surprise farewell dinner I threw him a week before he left.

I had told him that it was just the two of us going for

dinner to Diana Downtown, which was our entire gang's favourite restaurant in Guelph. We entered the diner and Zaid's jaw dropped when he saw a large, beautifully decorated table at the far end of the room. Fiona and Tia were holding up a colourful artwork banner that read: 'We'll miss you, Zaid!' The rest of the party comprised of Zaid's friends from his classes. I had considered inviting Arjun; I know he had sort of made things okay with Zaid. However, I didn't want to upset Fiona, so in the end I decided to leave him out.

Zaid hugged me tight and kissed me on the forehead. 'Thank you so much. This is great. You're the most thoughtful girlfriend ever. No one has ever thrown me a surprise party before,' he said, deeply moved.

'Aw! Well, this isn't a party; it's dinner. But yes, I am an amazing girlfriend, I know.'

He laughed and we walked to the table and greeted everyone there. It was a perfect night. After dinner, everyone went over to Zaid's apartment. We laughed as we played drinking games and recounted stories from this semester. And then, after everyone had left, I stayed behind, of course. Zaid and I cuddled and slept. I felt so safe in his arms. See, didn't I tell you it was the perfect night?

In some ways, the farewell night was better than the actual night before Zaid left. Zaid and I had dinner at Diana Downtown again, but this time around we were both sombre. We knew our time together was limited so the mood was one of pathos. After dinner, we went back to Zaid's apartment. When I entered his room, I burst into tears. It was as if the bare room finally drove home the message: Zaid was leaving. As in, I didn't know when I was going to see him again.

'Shh, baby. Don't cry, come on. It's going to be okay. I love you,' Zaid said tenderly as he drew me into his arms.

The 'L' word got my attention. I looked up at him. 'What? We had decided not to say "love", remember? It'll be all the harder to say goodbye now.'

'I don't care. I love you. And wouldn't want to leave without saying it.'

'I love you too. Of course, I do. I'm going to miss you so much.' I pulled him closer.

Before we knew it, it was morning. We had to take the bus to Toronto at 10 a.m. so Zaid could make it to the airport on time. We reached the airport sooner than I expected.

We stood at the entrance to the airport, hugging each other for what seemed like an eternity.

All morning, I kept telling myself to be strong and not cry. But when he kissed me and then squeezed my hand, I couldn't hold back my tears. 'Oh, my God. It's really happening. You're leaving.'

'I'll call you as soon as I reach home. And we'll Facetime. It's going to be okay, baby,' Zaid said, as his voice cracked and gave him away.

'No. This is the hardest thing I've ever had to do. I can't believe how much this hurts,' I replied.

Zaid hugged me tighter. I buried my face in his chest and inhaled his magical, musky scent.

'Baby, I've got to go now,' Zaid whispered, still hugging

me. I pretended I hadn't heard him. I knew I was being childish, but I couldn't help myself.

He pulled away after a few minutes. 'No matter how many times we say goodbye, it will never be enough, Rach. You have no idea how happy I am to have found you. You're my miracle. These last few months with you have been like a dream but we're the absolute "realest" real deal. I promise I'm going to find a way to come back to you. I don't want to lose you.'

I smiled through my tears. He kissed me one last time before he resolutely walked into the airport. I stood rooted to the spot, watching him fade into the crowd at the airport. I stood outside the airport for a long time. I don't know what I expected; I knew he wasn't coming back. I just stared into space replaying the first moment I saw him, the time he offered me his seat in the bus, the day he came to 'protect' me from Arjun's advances, the night at the club when he asked me out on a date, our coffee date, the night he stayed up to help me finish my assignment, our first kiss, Niagara, our fight, my apology ... the memories were endless. I smiled as I recalled the things he had said and done, I even laughed at one point. I'm sure the people around me thought I was nuts, but I honestly didn't give a damn.

Over the next few days, Precious, Fiona and Tia did their utmost to cheer me up. We went to the movies, to the mall, and even made a two-day girls-only trip to Quebec city. And then it was time for me to return home for my two-week break.

It has been great spending time with Mum, Dad, Aisha,

Amy and Jo. Zaid and I message each other throughout the day and Facetime for hours on end just before I go to bed. But even when I'm out at dinner with my family or hanging with my friends, my mind is constantly on Zaid. I've never been religious, but I haven't prayed this hard for anything in my life. I pray throughout the day so that God has no opportunity to ignore my prayer. If God exists, He'll have no option but to listen to my prayers and ensure that Zaid returns to Guelph for one more semester.

JANUARY

TIA

Neha and I are swaying our hips to '*Kala chashma*'. Neha smacks my butt and I giggle. I've been giggling incessantly all evening and realize I shouldn't have had so many shots, but, oh well, what can one do?

'Are we having a good time?' an upbeat Stan hollers over the mike.

'YES!' all two hundred of us chorus.

I have to admit for an amateur DJ, Stan is pretty amazing. He makes eye contact with us and motions us to join him at the bar on the opposite end of the room. Stan whispers something to his DJ partner, Rishi.

Neha and I make our way through the crowd to the bar.

Rishab's wedding has been an absolute riot. I'm so glad I made it. I'll be missing my first week back at campus, but I'm sure I'll make it up. It has been marvellous spending time with my friends again. And it has been especially great spending time with Armaan. The only issue is that he has been really busy managing the wedding arrangements.

Come to think of it, these last three weeks in India have been amazing. My relationship with my parents is finally the way I've always wanted it to be. They can see that living on my own has helped me grow responsible and so they've learned to trust me and let go. In the past, they would have asked a million questions before allowing me to make this trip to Goa for the wedding. However, now, they simply told me to go ahead and have a great time.

I remember the night that I landed in Mumbai. As soon as I saw my parents at the airport, I teared up. They both pulled me into their arms and we just stood there, a ball of emotion.

'I've missed you both so much. I love you,' I said, through my tears.

'We love you too, beta,' Ma said. 'So, so much. Welcome back home,' Pa added.

We stayed up talking until the wee hours; there was just so much to be said. Even though I had apologized to them for my behaviour over the phone after Thanksgiving weekend, there were some things which needed to be said in person. The next day, when I woke up, I went into the kitchen to make tea when Ma entered the kitchen wearing a surprised look.

'What are you doing?'

'Making *chai*. Why?'

'Nothing. Not used to seeing you in the kitchen,' Ma smiled.

When I handed her a cup of tea, she took a sip and said, 'Wah! This is really good *chai*.'

'Yeah, well, I've learned how to do my own chores. I've even learned how to make *dal chawal*.' I beamed.

Although I struggled with doing everything on my own initially, I quite enjoy doing my chores now. Everything except laundry.

I shared my laundry woes with Ma. 'We have separate washers and dryers in the laundry room in my res. Washing takes forty-five minutes. And drying another forty-five minutes. I usually put my clothes in the washer, go up to my room and then go back downstairs forty-five minutes later to transfer the clothes into a dryer. Anyway, I forgot my clothes in the washer this one time, and I only remembered when I woke up the next morning. When I went down to the laundry room, all my clothes were still there in the washer except for three of my pink tops. So, there's a pink-loving freak roaming the halls of my res! After that, every time I saw someone wear a pink T-shirt on campus, I'd look closely to see if it was mine! College is really mad. The craziest things happen and you meet the strangest people!'

Ma laughed at my story, but I could tell that she was impressed by how independent I had become.

I'm sipping water and staring at people shaking a leg on the dance floor when Armaan suddenly appears in front of us.

'Hey! Having fun?' he asks.

'Yes, this is the best sangeet I've ever been to! Well done on the organization,' I reply.

Armaan beams at me and I catch Neha and Stan exchanging a look. It was the same 'knowing' expression

Stan wore when we used to see Neha and Armaan together in the past.

'What?' I ask.

'Nothing.' Stan grins.

I can feel my cheeks getting warm.

Armaan on the other hand seems oblivious to Neha and Stan's expressions. Probably because he has been staring at me.

He clears his throat and says, 'Ti, you wanted to call your parents, right? Why don't we go to a quieter spot so you can make the call? We'll be back, guys,' he says to Neha and Stan.

Armaan holds my hand and leads me through the crowd. When we reach the hotel lobby, I look at him enquiringly. 'Where are we going?' I ask.

'You'll see,' he says with a glint in his eye.

What is going on?

We take the elevator up to the twelfth floor and then climb the flight of stairs to the hotel's rooftop restaurant, Breeze. A few couples are at the scattered tables, but otherwise the place is quiet. Or perhaps it feels quiet because we've just come from such a noisy venue. Armaan leads me to a candlelit table at the corner of the restaurant that overlooks the beach far below.

A smiling waiter pulls out our chairs for us.

'What is all this?' I ask, genuinely surprised.

'I saw you gazing at the picture of Breeze in the hotel guide. And I felt terrible about not being able to spend one-on-one time with you because of all this wedding stuff,' Armaan says, ruefully.

'But, are we actually going to have dinner here now? While your brother's sangeet is going on?'

'Why not? Everybody's busy drinking and dancing. No one will notice if we're missing for a bit. I realized we'll never get time together unless we steal some.' He smiles.

I reach across the table for his hand. I've never been this happy. This is the perfect moment. That's the best way to describe it. There's a nip in the air and I'm on a date with the perfect guy.

'Thanks, Armaan. For everything. For being so understanding and waiting patiently for me to figure out how I feel. And now, for this. This is the sweetest thing anyone has ever done for me. I ... um ... I've been thinking ... and I've finally decided.'

He looks expectantly at me. I look into his eyes and I just know. I've never been surer of anything in my life.

'My answer is yes! Yes, I want to be with you. Yes, I like you too. Like really, really like you. I'm just so in like with you, Armaan. I'm so happy I found you. But I also feel really stupid, you know. We were in the same circle, in the same city for three years and we didn't fall for each other. I mean, I used to see you every single day, for God's sake. And now, when I'm thousands of miles away from you, we'll be in a relationship! How is this even going to work?' I ask, exasperated.

'I know. Life is strange sometimes. But if you hadn't moved, we would never have bonded the way we did. Sometimes you need to step away to see what's right in front of you clearly. All I know is that things happen when the time is right. Also, you know how my parents always leave our summer holiday destination up to me? What do you think of, oh-I-don't-know, Canada for us this summer?' He winks.

'Oh, my God! Really? Yes! Yes! Yes! I'm already counting the days until Summer 2017!'

He laughs. And I beam at him. Armaan is right; there's no point in wondering why we didn't fall for each other sooner or worrying about our future. I need to live in the moment. And this moment, right now, is magical.

ZAID

Tap, tap, tap.

I can tune out the whooshing of the wind, courtesy of having lived on the eleventh floor for the last ten years. The incessant tapping, however, is rather annoying. Whoever is doing this, needs to stop. Now!

I glance to my left; the guy sitting two seats from me is completely engrossed in his phone. And then I catch a glimpse of my feet. Oh, God. I'm the one responsible for this infernal racket. It's a miracle the phone guy hasn't protested. I will my foot to stop tapping this very instant. It obeys. My phone beeps and as I extract it from my pocket, I realize my palms are sweaty. Why am I so nervous?

Oh, right. Because my happiness is wholly contingent on the outcome of this meeting. Ever since I saw the caller ID on my phone when it rang this morning, my heart hasn't stopped thumping. It was the International Students Office calling.

'Zaid Mahomed? Hi, Mbali here. I'm the new International Student Advisor. You've been in touch with Alicia Philips so far. Anyway, I'm calling to tell you that as per your request, we've sent your application to the University of Guelph for you to continue for one more semester as an exchange student. The University of Guelph accepts no more than twenty exchange students each semester from its various partner institutions across the world. So, your acceptance depends on the number of international students who have applied for their exchange programme for the coming semester. They are sorting through their applications as we speak and by this afternoon, we should know whether you have been accepted. If so, you will have to get signatures from the head of your department and the dean here at the university, just as you did last semester. However, you must get these signatures today because our offices will close down for the summer break which begins on Monday next week. Come to my office today at around 2.00 p.m. If you're accepted, we will ensure that you get all the requisite signatures today. Naturally, the form needs your signature as well. So, I guess I'll see you at my office this afternoon?'

I look at my watch. It's now 2.15 p.m. Mbali's secretary has informed me that she's on a call so I will need to wait. Although I've been outside this office for only twenty minutes, it feels like I've been waiting for a lifetime.

I take a deep breath. It's going to be okay. It *has* to be okay, I convince myself. I need a distraction. My phone beeps sadly to indicate I've forgotten to charge it: so I can't play a game or check social media to kill time. I make my way to the magazine rack by the reception desk. It's just as I reach for a brochure that I see her. She seems to be heading into the office adjoining Mbali's. She notices me at the same time and our eyes meet. Well, I couldn't have asked for a bigger distraction than this. I feel queasy.

Standing in front of me is Devi.

'Zaid! Hi! How are you?' she asks enthusiastically. It

was as if she had total amnesia about the cruel way she had bludgeoned my heart exactly a year ago.

I had envisioned this moment numerous times when I first moved to Canada, playing out various permutations of the scenario – bumping into her at the movies, at our favourite restaurant, or just seeing her on campus again. Back then I had thought the best way to get back at her would be to pretend that I had had the time of my life in Canada.

Now I realize, I won't have to pretend. I smile at her. 'Hi Devi! Long time! I'm great. How are you?'

She seems a little taken back by my nonchalance.

'Uh ... I'm great too. Can't complain. So ... uh ... how was Canada? I think it's really cool that you did the whole exchange thing. When Shana told me you were travelling, I couldn't believe it. I mean, you've never really been all that adventurous, you know.' I'm aware that she babbles when she's nervous.

'Canada was amazing. I'm so happy that I got the opportunity to go there. I met some fascinating people there and it completely changed my perspective on life. When you travel, you get to meet so many different people, from so many different walks of life, you know? And what's really amazing is how you end up finding things in common with them despite having such different backgrounds. Our similarities are so much stronger than our differences.' My smile widens as I think about Rach. 'Canada has been the best thing that has ever happened to me.'

Devi's jaw drops. Perhaps it was because I used to

tell her that she was the best thing that ever happened to me. I had meant it at the time, but I really didn't know any better. And then it suddenly hits me – I don't hate her anymore. My nausea has been replaced by relief. My resentment has been supplanted by supreme indifference. Devi no longer holds the reins to my life or has any bearing on my peace of mind. I'm finally free. Hate is as much of a burden to carry as unrequited love.

To be fair, I kinda met Rach because of Devi. If Devi hadn't broken my heart, I would never have travelled to Canada. And I would have missed out on the best time of my life.

'Uh … hey, I'm running late for my meeting with Prof. Moodley.' She gestures to the office adjacent to Mbali's. I'll see you around. Take care, Zaid.' There's an awkward moment where she contemplates hugging me. She finally decides to give me a quick wave before rushing into the professor's office.

'Zaid Mahomed?' the secretary calls out my name. 'You can go into Mbali's office now.'

I feel my nervousness dissipate. I've no idea what will happen next. But I know I'll be okay. I thought my life was over when Devi broke my heart a year ago, but it had really just been the beginning. 2016 has been the best year of my life. And something tells me no matter what happens everything will be okay. I know that I can handle anything that life throws my way. And I know that life is wonderful if you just let it unfold the way it's meant to.

ACKNOWLEDGEMENTS

I was an exchange student at the University of Guelph, Canada, when I was nineteen. Having grown up in South Africa, a country with an exceptionally high crime rate, it was no wonder that my parents were extremely protective of me.

The freedom I received living on campus at Guelph was unprecedented. Much like the nineteen-year-olds in this book, I treasured my independence. I had gone to Canada in search of new experiences and boy, did I get them. I loved meeting students from different parts of the world. I loved being exposed to new cultures. But most of all, I marvelled at how people with different cultural backgrounds could forge relationships. It made me realize that our similarities are much stronger than our differences.

I came back from that experience enriched. I'd share my love affair with Canada with anyone who'd listen. So in a way, I'd been carrying this story within me for ten years.

My previous books were about the messy twenties. But I wanted to go back in time and talk about being nineteen.

To everyone I met at Guelph; friends, student advisors and lecturers – thank you for the memories.

I'd like to thank my parents for their unconditional love and support. As a teenager, I know I couldn't wait to get away from home and chart my own path. Now that I live away from you, I miss you.

To my husband, Rohan, thank you for your belief in me and for your tough love! As always, you helped me get the job done.

Thanks to my in-laws, Ekta, Amrata, Amit and Roshan for the constant love and support.

Thank you to the HarperCollins team for believing in this book. Manasi Subramaniam, thank you, for first spotting the potential in the manuscript. Thank you Shantanu Chaudhuri, Prerna Gill and Swati Daftuar for making the book what it is.

And most importantly, thank you to my spiritual Guru for your guidance and blessings. Without you, I'd be lost.

HarperCollinsPublishersIndia

Subscribe to Harper Broadcast

Harper Broadcast is an award-winning publisher-hosted news and views platform curated by the editors at HarperCollins India. Watch interviews with celebrated authors, read book reviews and exclusive extracts, unlock plot trailers and discover new book recommendations on www.harperbroadcast.com.

Sign up for Harper Broadcast's monthly e-newsletter for free and follow us on our social media channels listed below.

Visit this link to subscribe: https://harpercollins.co.in/newsletter/

Follow us on

YouTube Harper Broadcast

Twitter @harperbroadcast

www.harperbroadcast.com

Follow HarperCollins Publishers India on

Twitter @HarperCollinsIN

Instagram @HarperCollinsIN

Facebook @HarperCollinsIN

LinkedIN HarperCollins Publishers India

www.harpercollins.co.in

Address

HarperCollins Publishers India Pvt. Ltd
A-75, Sector 57, Noida, UP 201301, India

Phone: +91-120-4044800